Adios, Nirvana

by Conrad Wesselhoeft

Houghton Mifflin
Houghton Mifflin Harcourt
Boston New York 2010

"Every moment of light and dark is a miracle."

—Walt Whitman

Houghton Mifflin is an imprint of Houghton Mifflin
Harcourt Publishing Company.

www.hmhbooks.com

The text of this book is set in Adobe Garamond.
Book design by Susanna Vagt

Library of Congress Cataloging-in-Publication Data
Wesselhoeft, Conrad.
Adios, Nirvana / Conrad Wesselhoeft.
p. cm.
Summary: As Seattle sixteen-year-old Jonathan helps a dying man come to terms with a tragic event
he experienced during World War II, Jonathan begins facing his own demons, especially the death of
his twin brother, helped by an assortment of friends, old and new.
ISBN 978-0-547-36895-5
[1. Death—Fiction. 2. Friendship—Fiction. 3. Grief—Fiction. 4. Musicians—Fiction. 5. Guitar—
Fiction. 6. High schools—Fiction. 7. Schools—Fiction. 8. Seattle (Wash.)—Fiction.] I. Title.
PZ7.W5166Adi 2010
[Fic]—dc22   2010006759

Manufactured in the United States of America
DOC 10 9 8 7 6 5 4 3 2 1
4500247739

For Claire, Kit, and Jen, with love

chapter 1

"Hey, man, get down!"

"Dude, don't be an idiot!"

It's my thicks calling to me. They're standing just off the bridge, in the little park with the totem pole. The one that looks out over Elliott Bay and downtown Seattle.

But tonight you can't see a thing. Tonight, the world is a giant shaken snow globe. Big flakes tumbling down. The size of potato chips.

In this city of eternal rain—snow! Once-a-decade snow. Maybe even once-a-century. It's piling fast.

We've been tossing frozen grapes at each other's open orifices. Kyle is extremely good at this—can catch a grape in his mouth at fifty feet. So can Javon. They dart and dive and roll, catching nearly every grape despite the swirly snow and patchy street light.

Nick and I pretty much suck.

I dig the grapes out of the snow. Eat them.

They are Mimi's little specialty, cored and filled with vodka. One or two or ten don't do much, but thirty or forty—*whoa!* Kyle lifted the whole bag from my freezer. I've had . . . god knows. I lost count a long time ago.

And now I'm feeling it. All of it. I'm spinning. Delirious. A little sick.

Plus, I gotta piss.

I'm standing on the rail of the bridge, midspan, grasping the light pole.

It's an old concrete bridge. The rail is waist high and just wide enough for me to perch on without slipping, as long as I hold on to the light pole.

I gaze up into the blazing industrial bulb. See the flakes lingering in the little upswirl. Below, the ground is bathed in perfect white darkness. It's not all that far down, twenty or thirty feet. Just enough to break a few bones—or kill you. It looks like a soft pillow. Dimpled by shrubs and bushes.

"Dude, dude, dude . . ."

"What're ya doin', man?"

I unzip and explode, blast a twelve-foot rope of steaming piss into the night.

When you piss off a bridge into a snowstorm, it feels like you're connecting with eternal things. Paying homage to something or someone. But who? The Druids? Walt Whitman? No, I pay homage to one person only, my brother, my twin.

In life. In death.

Telemachus.

Footsteps crunch up behind me. I know it's Nick—"Nick the Thick."

"Hey, Jonathan." His voice is quiet. "C'mon down."

Just then, my stomach churns. I tighten my grip on the light pole, lean out over the bridge. My guts geyser out of me. I taste the grapes, the soft bean burrito I had for lunch. The tots. The milk.

Twisting and drooling, I see below that spring has bloomed on the snow-covered bushes. Color has returned to the azaleas.

Another wave hits me. And another. All those damn grapes. And, god knows, more burrito and tots.

Till I'm squeezed dry.

Pulped out.

Empty.

I watch snowflakes cover my mess. It's like we're making a Mexican casserole together, the night and me. Night lays down the flour tortilla, I add the vegetable sauce.

When I look around, Kyle and Javon are standing there, too.

Kyle says, "If you break your neck, dude, I will never forgive you."

Javon says, "Already lost one of you. Get your ass down, or I'll drag it down."

It hurts. They are my oldest friends, my thicks.

And thickness is forever.

But somewhere in that snowy world below, Telemachus waits.

I loosen my grip on the light pole.

"Hey!" they shout. "HEY!"

My frozen fingers slip. Their panicky hands lunge for me.

But I'm too far gone.

I'm falling . . . falling. There's ecstasy and freedom here. Somehow I flip onto my back, wing my arms, Jesus-like, and wait for my quilty azalea bed to cradle me. And my Mexican casserole to warm me.

I fall, fall, fall into the snowy night.

Thinking of my brother.

Thinking of Telemachus.

chapter 2

An angel is peering down. Dressed all in white. Everlasting worry creases her forehead.

When she opens her mouth, I smell unfiltered Camels. Her halo hair is a slummy orange. Her white gown is a silk kimono—the one with the fiery dragon on the back.

"*Gawwwdddd,* Jonathan!" she sneers. "You *reek* of puke!"

She flings open the curtains. Outside, the trees and rooftops are caked in white. Snow is still falling. It calls to me. I'd answer, but I'm wired for sleep. I flap the quilt over my head.

"You're lucky you didn't get yourself killed, Jonathan. Or freeze to death. If it wasn't for Nick and Kyle and Javon . . ."

I have a vague memory of being lifted out of a snowy bush and stuffed into the back of Kyle's brother's ancient VW bug.

"They say you fell twenty feet—twenty feet!"

The angel is none other than the Reverend Miriam Jones. Mimi. My mom.

"How the hell did you fall off a bridge, Jonathan?"

"Go away, Mimi."

Here it comes . . .

"Jonathan, Jonathan, when are you gonna fix your life?"

Mimi's been asking me this for sixteen years. Since the day I popped out, two minutes and twelve seconds behind Telly, and winked at her.

"Next Tuesday," I say.

"Jonathan, Jonathan," Mimi says, pulling back the quilt and planting her face in mine. "Doesn't your mother have enough to cry about?"

I have a headache that begins in my tailbone, pulses up my spine, and plays "Purple Haze" in my sixth and ninth vertebrae. My mouth's a bag of cotton. My eye bones ache.

I stretch my arms and legs, test my fingers and toes, roll my neck. I'm not broken, but I feel like I've been flattened by the Green Bay defense.

"*Gawwwdddd,*" Mimi says. "I can't even get down to the Bean."

Mimi's a barista at the Bikini Bean Espresso Drive-Thru. Their slogan is way more effective than anything Starbucks ever used:

"Only one string attached."

I wrote that line.

Based on all the truckers and welders that jammed the window lane after they posted the sign, I should've gotten paid *at least* one thousand dollars. Instead, they paid me in caffeine— one frickin' latte, and not even a venti.

Writers *never* get paid what they're worth.

"Take the sled," I say.

Mimi coughs, like a trucker.

"There's a letter for you, Jonathan."

She snaps the envelope against her ass.

"Not now, Mimi. Go away."

She dangles the envelope in front of me. "It's from Dr. Jacobson."

Thwack!

Gupti the Witch. The last person I want to hear from: the

principal at Taft High School, a six-foot-two Indian from Mumbai. I can't think of her without hearing sitar music or smelling saffron rice. I've been expecting her hammer to fall for weeks.

Sleep is pulling hard. Beautiful little sirens. Pixie dancers. Four or five Tinkerbells. But they tremble at the sound of Mimi's voice. *Poof!* Gone.

"Look at this room! *Gawwwdddd!* It's bombed-out Baghdad in here. Why must you throw your T-shirts on the curtain rods? And pick up your damn books! My god, Jonathan, why are you so hard on your books?"

It's true, I *am* hard on my books. You don't get your money's worth till you've slammed them against the wall a few times. Broken their backs. My books are my family—the more they hurt me, the more I hurt them. My most hurtful, beaten book is *Leaves of Grass* by Walt Whitman. Telly gave it to me on our fifteenth birthday, scrawling these words inside the cover:

CONTRADICT YOURSELF.
CONTAIN MULTITUDES.
SEE YOU IN SKATER HEAVEN.

Now, there was a visionary.

"And what happened to your guitar?" Mimi says.

She slips her fist through the splintered hole. "You and Telly used to play such sweet things for me, Jonathan. Why don't you play 'American Pie' anymore?"

My guitar, Ruby Tuesday, is the unrivaled queen of my room. She's a six-string Larrivée acoustic, a pretty Canadian from up-country Saskatchewan with a nasty hole just south of the pick guard. What happened? Kyle's oafy foot happened.

"Didn't you pay something like five hundred dollars on eBay for this guitar?"

"Three eighty."

"You're always throwing your money away, Jonathan."

Like hell. Ruby's worth every penny, even with the extra hole. She's tattooed with lines of poetry—a mix of my own, Whitman's, and others'—plus autographs and snide Kyle-isms. And she always smells nice—the scent of ancient forests, lavender, and tacos. Right now, she sits in my rocking chair wearing my North Face vest. She's the only girl I put my arms around.

Mimi fires up a Camel. Then she slips the letter from the envelope, unfolds it.

"Open your ears, baby."

"Jeezus, Mimi."

" 'Dear Jonathan . . . Miss Sosa informs me . . .' "

I bury myself in my quilt, press my hands against my ears, create my own soundproof chrysalis. Mimi steps up to my bed, bends over. Her voice cuts through the chrysalis fibers and I hear every one of Gupti's words.

" '. . . that, as of today, you have missed sixteen consecutive Spanish III classes. I checked with Mr. Maestretti, and apparently you have not attended physics for eight of the past ten days. In history and math, your grades are, respectively, anemic and dire. Only Dr. Bramwell, in American Lit, reports that you are doing good work. For a student who showed so much promise one year ago—and who bathed our school in glory last October—this is a major disappointment. The tragic loss of your brother . . .' "

Mimi gasps. A sob bursts inside her. I respect it. Lie totally still. For a millisecond, nothing separates us. I even ponder putting an arm around her. She takes a deep breath and keeps reading.

" '. . . does not alter certain facts about your education. Here is one hard fact to consider: on your present course, you will not be promoted to the twelfth grade in June. Please come to my office Monday fourth period prepared to discuss your strategy for success. Sincerely, Gupti R. Jacobson, PhD, principal, William Howard Taft High School, West Seattle.' "

Mimi paces back and forth. Mumbling.

If Gupti is my enemy, I do have a friend: Dr. Robert Bramwell (a.k.a. "Birdwell"). He's my champion. But he's also a hemorrhoid. Because of him, I'm famous. Because of him, people think I'm a prodigy. They expect me to pull a rabbit out of a hat. Part the Red Sea. Win the Nobel Prize.

Telemachus got hit on April 17. He died twenty-five days later, on May 12, at 2:11 a.m. at Harborview Medical Center. In June, Birdwell entered my poems in the Quatch—Washington State's best-young-poet competition—and in October I won. Beat out students nineteen years old, twenty, twenty-one, including guys majoring in creative writing at the University of Washington. And here I was, barely sixteen. In all the Quatch's thirty-nine-year history, the judges had never picked anybody so young.

All hell broke loose.

ALL HELL.

A tidal wave of fame lifted me out of the backwater kelp, flung me onto the sand. They flicked on the bright lights. Everybody smiled, except for the losers.

"Birdwell called this morning," Mimi says. "He got a copy of the letter. He has an idea."

"*Holy jeezus!* Leave me alone, Mimi."

She pulls back the quilt. "A job, Jonathan."

Her lips curl pleasurably around the sound of those words. "It's got *white collar* written all over it."

"It's six a.m. Let me sleep."

"It's eleven eighteen a.m.," Mimi says. "Get your sorry poetic ass out of bed!"

"Bring me some orange juice," I say.

"A little money on the side, Jonathan."

"Get me some goddamn orange juice, Mimi!"

She swishes out of my room and comes back with a mug of tap water. It's an old coffee mug, and she hasn't bothered to wash it. Globs of scum float on the surface.

"It would be more than I could pay you," she says.

For the past five months, my job has been to prime and paint the house. It's what I do every Saturday and Sunday. Stand on scaffolding, sand, and chip. All day, rain or shine.

Painting is phase one in Mimi's grand plan to convert our house into a wedding chapel: "The Chapel of the Highest Happiness." Once I get the primer done, I'm supposed to paint the house purple. We'll be the pride of Delridge Avenue. Mimi'll dress in her white minister robe, put on *Songs of the Humpback Whale,* and marry people of all shapes and shades—midgets and giants, angels and murderers—in a cloud of incense and plastic roses.

Mimi pays me nothing for weeks, then suddenly waves a few twenties in my face. With her, it's feast or famine. But it never adds up to minimum.

At the rate I'm going, I'll break the seal on the first can of purple in about twenty-five years. Mimi wants it done by

June 1, in time to catch the wedding season.

"How'm I gonna do a second job?"

"Whatever it takes, baby," she says. "Cut back on sleep."

I sip the rancid water. "What's the job?"

"Writer," Mimi says, picking a tobacco nit off her tongue.

"Writer?"

"Some dying old man wants somebody to write his life story. Or something like that. I'm not sure. You'll have to speak with Birdwell."

"You gotta be joking."

Mimi leans close, revealing too much under her kimono. I close my eyes.

"Cross my heart, baby. I'm not joking. Birdwell nominated you."

A flame flares to life, but I don't show it. I deepen my frown.

These days, I seem to disappoint everybody except Birdwell. For some reason, he won't give up on me. In his classroom, he's tacked the *Seattle Times* article about me next to posters of Jack Kerouac and Mark Twain, two other writers who lost brothers. He's also tacked up two of my poems, "Opaque Miracles" and "The Day I Saw a Sasquatch."

Back in October, I rode that wave. Now I'm through with fame. All I want is to rest, get some sleep. Sleep for a thousand years. The lesson of fame is simple: it sucks. My advice to anyone who wants to be famous: stay obscure, and get a good night's sleep.

"Birdwell thinks you're god's gift to creation, Jonathan. I think he's in love with you."

"Go away, Mimi."

"Baby, get out of bed and go talk to him."

"Are you crazy? I nearly died last night!"

"My poor little boy," she says. "Somehow you managed to survive."

Classic Mimi. Sixteen years, and she still doesn't know the first goddamn thing about being a mom.

"I beg you," I say. "Go away. And put some clothes on."

Mimi tightens the belt on her kimono. Smiles. "I'll give you one hour, baby."

I pull the sheet over my head. It's 11:25 a.m., but it feels like midnight.

I sink quickly.

chapter 3

I'm standing at the bus stop, sipping a can of Red Bull and shivering in my favorite hoodie—a black zip-up with ESPAÑA stamped across the chest. Over that, I'm wearing a flannel shirt, looking like a real Northwest logger. Better yet, looking like the great grunge rock god Eddie Vedder, of West Seattle and the world. My boxers ride my bellybutton. My Levi's ride my butt crack.

The world is falling in curtains of white. A Jeep Cherokee bombs down the street, kicking up a rooster ass of snow, spraying all the two-wheel drives hibernating in their curbed snow caves.

I'm at home in this world—this clash of innocence and arrogance, elves and idiots. If only Walt Whitman would walk up and stand here, all pink-cheeked and gray-bearded in his floppy hat. He, too, had a brother who got hurt. He, too, sat in the hospital, night after night. We'd have a lot to talk about, Walt and me.

The pitter-patter of nurses' feet.

The gaping void of tomorrow.

In the back of my throat I can still taste last night's grapes. Feel the rawness.

I drain my Red Bull and smile at the memory of my fall. Twenty feet—damn!—and not a broken bone. I know my thicks will spread the word. Jonathan—poet and superman.

It's not how I see myself; I'm just a poet. Nothing dual about that. But they're always spreading the word, building my legend.

"I'm Jonathan, not Telly," I say. "Let me be forgotten."

They ignore me.

Most things are out of my control anyway, as the world has taught me.

Only twenty feet? It seemed like a lot more. Somehow, I know there's a connection between my fall and the snow, between me and Walt Whitman, between Whitman and Telly. But I can't quite figure it out. That's what poetry is for, building those connections. When I figure it out, I'll put it in my new poem, "Tales of Telemachus."

So far, "Tales of Telemachus" stands at 317 lines, and it's still growing.

I've divided it into sections, each of which I call a *chaos*.

Ezra Pound called each section in his long poem a *canto*.

Jack Kerouac called each section in *Mexico City Blues* a *chorus*.

I prefer *chaos* because there's no structure, no logic, to how I write.

I write fast. Free. Gut.

All my lines spring from some dark well.

Boiling with razor fish.

Ugly-lonely sturgeon.

Damselfish with ADD.

So far, "Tales of Telemachus" consists of twelve chaoses.

It's shaping up to be my masterpiece.

• • •

The No. 22 crunches around the corner, tires crisscrossed with giant snow chains. The driver, a beefy guy in a furry hat, pops the door. He grins when I show him my school pass.

"Is this heaven or what?"

"Yeah," I say. "Heaven."

The snow glues us like brothers, but only for two seconds.

I drop into a seat over a back wheel. Sprawl myself across the narrow heating vent. But as soon as the bus pulls out, I know I've chosen the wrong seat. Every spin of the wheel slams a tail of metal chain against the floor under my feet. My headache wakes up. My stomach kicks into tumble dry.

I slide to a nonthunking seat.

In the window of the No. 22, I am colorless—the corpse that could be lying in the morgue today, with a tag on his toe.

To climb onto the rail of a bridge and piss into the snow— hey, that's just marking your territory.

But to let go—that's insanity.

It scares the *holy jeezus* out of me.

chapter 4

Birdwell lives in a decayed tooth of a building called the Fauntleroy Arms. It's downtown, pretty far up Pine, by the Paramount Theatre.

A homeless man sleeps in a shadow, in the dry space under the Greek columns.

I dig in my shirt pocket for my pencil and little notebook. Let it flow fast. Not just because I have a headache, but because fast writing puts me in touch with my primal, sacred, universal self.

Chaos XIII

O sleeping bum of a building,
you cradle the litter of our streets
under your fake Doric columns.
You saw our grandfathers
stalk these sidewalks
in Humphrey Bogart hats
posing for blurry black-and-white photos.
Back in the basement years
when nuclear families huddled
against Khrushchev
and drank canned milk.
Gutter Hercules!

Go ahead,
shiver on your cardboard bed.
You have found your place
in history
under the quake-cracked columns,
stained with pigeon shit.
I search for mine.

I've squeezed in a reference to the Cuban Missile Crisis, which we're studying in Mr. Mandelheim's class. But I'm not too happy with some of the lines. For example, "quake-cracked" sounds like "quacked." And I'm not sure what a Doric column is.

I'll fix it later.

I take the elevator up to the fifth floor. Before I knock, I hear Birdwell cooing inside. We all have theories about Birdwell, and maybe now I can prove one of them.

When he opens the door, he's all smiles.

"Hello, Jonathan."

"Hey, Dr. Bird . . . Bramwell."

I glance over his shoulder.

Birdwell is a sparrow of a man. Beak nose. Thick glasses. Big, protruding chest. He has a funny way of walking, quick hipped.

His apartment is disgustingly clean. He isn't wearing shoes, only big wool socks, so I slip out of my puddly Nikes.

"Jonathan, you look like a truck ran over you."

"A forty-ton semi," I say. "Is somebody else here?"

"No, just you and me."

"But . . ."

"Ahh," he says, breaking into a grin. "C'mere, Janey!"

· 16 ·

I expect god knows what—a voluptuous transvestite or, at least, a yipping terrier—to bolt out of the bedroom.

Instead, a robot blinks to life, rolls over, and stops, facing Birdwell. The robot stands maybe two feet tall. She's built like Carmen Electra. Her name, Calamity Jane, is branded onto her tank top. Her bellybutton is showing. It's pierced. So is an eyebrow.

"Say hi to Jonathan, Janey."

"Hi, Jonathan." Her voice is sexy, in a robot-y way.

"Well, aren't you going to say hi back?" Birdwell asks me.

"Hi," I say.

Birdwell beams with joy.

"Now ask her what she thinks of you."

Whoa! This is creeping me out. But I'm his guest.

"Go on, ask."

"What do you think of me?"

"You're the sexiest man alive," Janey says.

Birdwell cracks up. So do I. But I'm pretty sure we're laughing for different reasons.

"Janey," he says, "is very good to me." He winks. "I mean good-good."

"Good-good?"

He nods. "She vacuums every morning after I leave for school and every night after I do the dishes. And she's a wonderful listener—no back talk. Not like my juniors and seniors. Nothing at all like you, Jonathan."

He smiles at the big-boobed little robot. "Thank you, my sweet. Bye-bye."

"Bye-bye," she says, and spins a 180, rolling over to a landing pad in the corner. She blinks ecstatically, then shuts down.

Birdwell glows like a proud father. Then his face darkens. He goes over to a side table and grabs his copy of Dr. Jacobson's letter. Holds it in my face.

"I trust you've seen this."

"Yeah."

I start to sit on his couch—a soft beige one with big pillows—but Birdwell screams, "Wait!" He pulls out a roll of bubble wrap and places it on the sofa, on my side. He does not put bubble wrap under himself.

We both sit, side by side, and the weight of my ass pops a few bubbles.

"Well?"

"Well what?"

"Do you have a strategy for success?"

I shrug. "Just live. Take it one day at a time. Be true to myself."

Birdwell sighs. "Jonathan, Jonathan . . . Listen to me:

'There is a tide in the affairs of men.
Which, taken at the flood, leads on to fortune . . .'"

He shakes a finger at me.

"*'Omitted, all the voyage of their life*
Is bound in shallows and in miseries . . .'

Do you know who wrote that?"

I shake my head.

"Take a guess."

"Christopher Columbus?"

"It was William Shakespeare. In *Julius Caesar*. Do you know what it means?"

"No."

"Take a guess."

ADIOS, NIRVANA

"We should all go on a Caribbean cruise?"

He glares at me. "Get serious, Jonathan!"

I shrug. "I have no idea what it means."

"It means," he says, "there are moments in life when one has to take action. These moments can be wonderful opportunities, but they're not always apparent to us. They often last a brief time—a few days, a few hours. Once they've past, they're gone forever. Here is your moment, Jonathan. A chance to do what you do best: write. And get paid for it."

"How much?"

He waves the thought away, like a fart. "Irrelevant. It doesn't matter."

"It matters to me."

"Then you ask the question," Birdwell says. "I did, however, make inquiries."

Inquiries. I roll the word around. It's a headache-y word, very "admin." I've never used it. Never will. Unless maybe in a poem, as a dagger.

"A man named David Cosgrove lives in a hospice in the Admiral District. He wants to pay someone to write a book about his life. Specifically, he wants you, Jonathan."

"Me!"

Birdwell nods. "He caught you on TV. Apparently someone downloaded your poems for him. He liked two of them."

"Oh, yeah? Which ones?"

Birdwell scratches his memory. "'Baboonery' and 'Blood-curdling Cliché.'"

"And all the others sucked?"

Birdwell shrugs. "Fame opens doors, Jonathan."

"Slams them shut, too," I say.

· 19 ·

Birdwell leans close and blows a puff of air into my eyes—his very weird way of telling me to shut up.

"You need to know, Jonathan, that Mr. Cosgrove has a few medical issues."

"What kind of medical issues?"

"Heart disease," Birdwell says. "And cancer."

"Heart disease *and* cancer?"

Birdwell nods. "And he's blind."

"*Whoa!* Dude, I'm not going within a mile of anybody like that."

Birdwell blinks. "Why not?"

"For one," I say, "I'm not into illness. For two, I don't like hospitals. For three, four, and five, I don't like old people who smell like piss. I don't like anything about any of this. It makes me sick. The answer is no!"

Birdwell shakes his head. "Jonathan, you're too young to carry so many biases. To be so *anti*."

"Hey," I say, "I wouldn't peer through a smoky glass window into that world. Not even if he paid me double minimum."

"He just might," Birdwell says. "He's an interesting old man, Jonathan. A veteran of World War Two. An award-winning journalist."

"A journalist! Why doesn't he write his own damn book?"

"Well, possibly because he's blind. And possibly because he wants someone impartial, with fresh eyes."

I goggle him. "Look into these eyes. They're as rancid as old cheese."

"I told him you are 'brilliant' and 'personable.' Half of that is true."

"Which half?"

"Jonathan, he's willing to pay you to write a book about his life."

"Tell him to hire a real writer."

"You *are* a real writer!"

"Hey, I'm not a real anything. Just because I won that stupid contest—"

"Oh, stop it, Jonathan! I'm doing you a favor. If you can't see that . . . Listen, it's a writing job. Not one of your house-painting or grease-monkey jobs. A writing job! I've been teaching for eighteen years, and in all that time there have been maybe five students—no, maybe three—I'd recommend for this, and you are definitely one. Besides, aren't you always telling me you're broke? Aren't you always heading off to rob the Wells Fargo stagecoach? Think of it as a chance to get raw material for your poems."

"*Whoa!*" I say. "Don't go there. I've got fourteen lifetimes' worth of raw material."

"Yes, yes," Birdwell says tiredly. "Your existential angst is all very impressive. The point is, Jonathan, if you do this—and do it to a satisfactory conclusion, and *honorably*—I can get you off the hook with Dr. Jacobson."

Finally, he has my attention.

"How can you do that?"

"Well, if we play our cards right, you won't be held back next year. This is a very special opportunity, Jonathan. A *compensatory* project."

"Compensatory?"

"Yes," Birdwell says. "I'm proposing that this be equal to all the work you've missed. A way to pay back the school. But you must embrace the project. You must commit, Jonathan. Nothing half-baked."

"Hey," I say, "when I commit, I bake it all the way, at four hundred twenty-five degrees."

All through this yabbering something inside me is sinking. I'm supposed to be painting the house, and I'm way behind. I have no room in my life for another job. No time to write somebody else's book. All of my inner architecture—all the screws, bolts, and steel beams—is needed to hold up my own life, writing "Tales of Telemachus," hanging out with my thicks, messing with Ruby Tuesday. Oh yeah, and school—can't forget that.

Somewhere in there I'm trying to squeeze a girlfriend. And work on my virginity issues.

And I'm about three years behind on sleep.

"This old man, does he wear diapers?"

Birdwell jumps up and goes to his desk. He grabs an envelope and hands it to me. I study the address:

David O. H. Cosgrove II
Delphi House
327 East Fillmore St. SW
Seattle, WA 98116

Inside is a one-paragraph letter about my incredible personality and literary genius. Birdwell has signed it with a loopy flourish. Like a twelve-year-old girl.

He purses his lips. "Do you know what a hospice is, Jonathan?"

"Yeah, it's where sick old people in diapers go to tank."

Birdwell sighs. "It's a sanctuary for the terminally ill."

"Everybody there's gonna die, right?"

"We're all going to die, Jonathan."

"Not me," I say. "Least, not in one of those places. I'll jump off a bridge before that happens."

Birdwell frowns. He doesn't know about my little bridge escapade, but I'm sure he'll find out. He always does.

I try to hand him back the envelope. "Look," I say, "you know where I'm coming from."

He grabs my elbow, walks me to the door.

"Go see David Cosgrove, Jonathan. Talk with him. See what kind of book he wants you to write. After all, you're the best young writer in the state of Washington, are you not?"

"Best poet," I say. "There's a difference."

Birdwell slips the envelope into the pocket of my flannel shirt.

"There is a tide in the affairs of men, Jonathan," he says. "This is your tide. Ride it, man."

"I'll ride it tomorrow," I say. "After I wax my surfboard."

Birdwell shakes his head. "Now's when the iron's hottest."

I nod toward the window. "In case you haven't noticed, the iron's not too hot."

"Goodbye, Jonathan."

"Adios," I say.

chapter 5

I hike down to the Pike Place Market. A scraper truck rumbles by and heaves a wave of snow onto the curb. It's no longer pure white. Now there's grit and soot mixed in. A sign of reality. The only other sound's the crunch-crunch of my Nikes.

At the market, the newsstand guy stands in bulging layers of sweaters. He and the miniature-doughnut lady and two white-coated fishmongers stare blankly into the cold. One of the fish-mongers catches my eye. "Fresh coho!" he cries.

Just what I need—fresh coho.

If you blot out the modern crap—the background cars and glass buildings—the market is framed by another century. It's London in the 1800s, and there's a big hooked goose waiting for the Cratchit family. Charles Dickens is writing all this by candlelight right up there in the garret window.

And that gray man in the seedy overcoat is Walt Whitman. And that greasy man with the bulbous nose outside the pizza window is Charles Bukowski. And we're all coming together here at the market to drink coffee and talk about writing and death.

That's what snow does. It opens a window in the mind, and everything crisscrosses and intersects: stories, centuries, people. Maybe if I look hard enough—like around the corner and behind the crab crates—I'll even see Telly.

I board the southbound 22. The same fat driver is at the

wheel. Now he's tired and says nothing. He doesn't celebrate the snow. We're definitely not brothers.

I take a seat halfway back on the right, nowhere near the thunking chains. I open my little notebook, fish out my stubby pencil. Scrawl:

Chaos XIV
The difference between snow and rain ...
Snow is me and Telly
poppin' the five-stair
behind Taft High School,
heel-flipping over the rail
behind Taco Time,
shredding Highland Hill.
Rain is hiding
behind Vic's garage,
surrounded by old tires,
shivering, back to back.
Snow is me and Telly
racing down Delridge
to drop our lines in Longfellow Creek.
Rain is standing at his bedside
watching the saline drip.

On the West Seattle Bridge, some cars spin out, bang into each other, pinball, and slide to a stop, fenders interlocked, blocking the lanes. We grind to a halt. Our driver's neck turns purple, but—well-trained Metro driver that he is—he doesn't cuss or anything, though I know he wants to.

Soon I hear "blurp-blurp-blurp." A cop car cruises past, flashing red and blue. It stops beside us. The cop gets out, sticks his head into the bus. "A tow truck's on the way," he says. "For your own safety, do not leave the bus."

That's my cue. As soon as he's gone, I walk to the front of the bus. The door is open, for air, and I step right out.

"Hey, what the . . . ? Get back in!" the driver barks.

But I keep going and don't look back. I hike past the jammed cars out onto the open freeway. I've never walked on a freeway before, let alone in the snow, let alone on a giant arched bridge over a river.

The cop doesn't notice at first. He's talking to drivers. I go about fifty yards, and then I hear him shouting. He gets on his loudspeaker and pelts me with threats. I don't care because I know he won't follow me. His car's trapped. And he's not about to chase me down on foot.

It's beautiful up on the bridge—gusts of white wind, tumbling facefuls of snow. It's a hundred times worth the cop threats.

I hike over to the guard rail, which is exactly testicle high, and just stand there, my Nikes planted firmly on slick ice. It's at least a hundred and fifty feet down to the Duwamish River. The water looks black. No question about it, the river is death. I'm only one slip away from Telemachus.

One slip away from the great *Adios!*

I close my eyes. Open my arms.

Man, it's so peaceful up here.

I let the gusts tilt me back and forth.

Then I jerk and jump back to safety.

God knows, Mimi's been through enough. And my thicks—

Kyle, Javon, Jordan, and Nick—how can I do this to them? We were chubby babies in preschool together. And now we are lean, shaggy, guitar-playing, skateboarding, video-gaming, grape-tossing brothers. Even though our leader is gone. Even though he's in skater heaven.

My motto—Never compromise—came from him.

Most of my best thoughts and memories came from him.

I popped my first stairs because of him.

I play guitar because of him. Not as well as he did technically, but I can make it howl. I can make it weep.

I am a poet because of him. He got me started on Whitman. Got me going on Bukowski—"Uncle Buk."

God bless you, Telly.

But I can't do this.

Even though Whitman wrote:

> *Nothing can happen*
> *More beautiful than death.*

At least, not today.

On the other side of the hump, I start skating. At first, I'm a little shaky and go only a short distance. Then I find a frozen tire groove and start running. I take off and blast down the ice. All the drivers in the oncoming lanes stare bug-eyed as I skate down the long span of the freeway bridge. On the wings of Nikes.

I've got a decision to make. The first exit is Delridge Way, which will take me home. A bit later is Admiral Way, which will take me to Diaper Man. I'm wired from my flight down the West Seattle Bridge. But I'm also tired—tired in a way that will take more than a few hours' sleep to fix.

"I'm doing this for you, Birdwell," I say, hiking past the Delridge exit and aiming toward Admiral Way. "For you, too, William Shakespeare."

chapter 6

By the time I reach Delphi House, I've walked ten miles. Okay, I've actually walked only four miles, but the snow makes it feel like ten. The whole time, night is slinking in, but it never gets dark. Just deeper shades of milky gray.

The Delphi is a cinder block structure. Basic kindergarten design.

I push inside and am sucked into a stream of smells: lemon air freshener, medicine, cancer, piss. It's putridly, stomach-turningly foul, a foul that soaks your spirit, weakens everything, saps life. Worst of all, it's the smell of false hope. Put that in a piñata, and I'll smash it with a bat. It's my moral duty.

The urge to turn around and walk out is strong. I'm against everything this place stands for: Wheelchairs, breathing tubes, oxygen tanks, comas, clipboards, waiting to die. I saw it all with Telemachus. I'd like to bulldoze it into a giant iron box, weld it tight, and drop it into the deepest part of the ocean.

But the spirit of the unholy trinity—Gupti, Birdwell, and Mimi—shoves me forward. I think about Shakespeare's tide, how it has washed me here. Flung me like a flopping fish onto the sand.

Two receptionists glance up. One is potato-faced. I can't see her ass, but I know it's about the size of a flat-screen TV. The other is . . . hmm . . . eighteenish, maybe even sixteenish, with long dreadlocked twists of hair and light green eyes. Maybe she's Asian, maybe black. Hell, maybe Arapaho or Nicaraguan—or maybe all of them. A global smoothie.

Just as I plant my hands on the counter, a buzzer rings. Flat Ass rises like a biscuit and floats away.

This leaves Dreadlock staring at me.

"I'm here to see one of your patients," I say.

"Guests," she says. "Everybody here is a guest. We have no patients."

I point to a woman dozing in a wheelchair a few yards away. She's hooked to an oxygen tank and some kind of drip pouch. "She's a guest?"

Dreadlock nods. "Mmm-hm."

We go eyeball to eyeball. I can beat those green marbles. Then I notice she, too, is sitting in a wheelchair. So I blink. Fumble in my pocket for Birdwell's letter, hand it to her.

"Do you have a *guest* named David O. H. Cosgrove the Second?"

"We do." She studies the letter. Looks up, puzzled.

"You're the writer?"

"Hey," I say, puffing out my chest. "I'm the poet. The wanderer at midnight."

I slip into my patter.

"I hear America singing.
When she sings out of tune,
I tickle her nose with a pigeon feather.
I smash her conscience
with a ball-peen hammer."

Dreadlock's mouth curves into a smile. The chill in her eyes melts, but only a drop.

"Walt Whitman you are not," she says.

Whoa!

My patter is based on Whitman—his "I Hear America Singing" stuff. It's an inverse, Yoda-esque style of writing:

I hear America singing,
The varied carols I hear . . .

"You know Whitman?" I ask.

"What are you, twelve years old?"

"Eighteen," I lie.

"Are you really the guy in this letter?"

I slip back into my patter:

"I am the beacon of hope,
the messenger of the pope.
I will free you with my rope
and wash you with my soap."

I'm pretty sure Dreadlock hasn't seen anybody like me for a while. If I'm lucky, she'll banish me from the building. That would be a good thing.

"You're not the only poet around here," she says. "C'mon, I'll introduce you."

She flips open the door on the countertop, wheels out, pops a turn.

We roll down the corridor. At room 114, she brakes. "Quiet!" she whispers.

Inside, a night-light casts a glow of lavender death. It smells like a tropical garden—a little too ripe.

Dreadlock squeezes the hand of the old woman lying in bed. "Agnes . . . Agnes . . ."

The old woman jerks. Her eyes open. She is truly old—Guinness Book of Records old.

"Look who's here," Dreadlock says.

A little waterfall gurgles in the corner. A standing fan breezes back and forth. The old woman waves for me to come closer. She reaches out, grabs my wrist, walks her brittle fingers over my knuckles, pulls my hand to her cheek.

In a trembly voice, she says, "You've come to bind up our wounds."

"Nah," I say. "Just visiting."

"You have work to do," she says.

"Yeah," I say. "You got that right."

"Go down to the sea," Agnes says. "Free the swimmers in the dark."

Whoa! This old lady *is* a poet.

"Where is your lute?" the old woman says.

"My lute?"

"I want you to play for me."

"Hey, I don't have a lute."

"Next time," Dreadlock says. "He'll play for you next time."

"Float a turd," Agnes says.

Coming from such ancient lips, this little diamond is so pure that it shines a light in the dimness. I feel better already.

Agnes relaxes her grip on me. Her fingers fall.

Out in the corridor, I say, "Is this what you do for fun around here?"

"She knew you'd come today," Dreadlock says. "She's been talking about it for weeks."

"Hey, even I didn't know I was coming till about an hour ago."

Dreadlock brakes her wheelchair. "Do you believe in second vision?"

"Second vision?"

"Prophecy."

"Hey, I'm a poet. I believe in everything."

"Well, try believing in this," Dreadlock says. "Agnes is supposed to be in the advanced stages of dementia. But if you listen carefully and dissect her words, they start to make sense. Her mind isn't gone; it's in a different place. Maybe even a beautiful place. Who's to say she's not better off than we are? I call her the Oracle at the Delphi."

"Like in ancient Greece?"

"Yeah," Dreadlock says. "Like the prophetess who foretold the future for Alexander the Great."

"And you think Agnes can foretell the future?"

Dreadlock eyeballs me from her wheelchair. "What's your name again?"

"Jonathan."

"You're real quick, Jonathan."

We roll up to room 101. The nameplate on the wall outside the door says DAVID COSGROVE. Dreadlock pokes her head inside. "You have a visitor, David."

She shoves me into the room. Pulls the door shut.

Click!

Now I'm standing alone, facing David O. H. Cosgrove II. He's propped up in his hospital bed. He turns his head.

"Jonathan, is that you?"

"Yeah."

"Well, it's about time."

chapter 7

David is long and stringy, old and tanned. But his tan is not healthy. He is kidney-bean bald. His eyes are the cloudy earth as seen from the moon.

"I follow the news," he says, waving a finger at the TV. "Seems you've had quite a season."

"A season?"

He nods, feels a sneeze coming on, gropes wildly for the Kleenex box. He misses and sneezes a magnitude ten onto his pajama sleeve. His hands find the Kleenex, and he grabs a wad. Blows. The room rattles with the thunderous unclogging of mucous passageways.

"A season of tragedy and triumph," David says, polishing his nose. "I'm sorry about your brother, Jonathan."

"Yeah."

Even that much is too personal. I fight the urge to walk out.

"That literary prize—somebody compared you to a high school quarterback ready to enter the NFL. Is that a good analogy?"

"Not really," I say. "I wrote a few poems, that's all."

"Let me turn this off."

He fumbles with the remote and clicks off the TV.

"Sit down, Jonathan."

I find a folding chair in the corner, open it, sit.

"I'm looking for somebody to help me tell my story."

"Why not tell it yourself?"

He smiles. "I've tried, but it doesn't come out right."

"Weren't you a journalist a long time ago?"

"Yes," he says. "Sometime back in the eighteenth century."

I shrug. "Just talk into a tape recorder. Get somebody to type it up."

He shakes his head. "That's not writing."

"I'm not cheap."

David Cosgrove frowns. "Of course not, Jonathan. Your fees have obviously gone up as a result of winning the Nobel Prize."

"That's right," I say.

There's a dinner tray on the side table, but the food is barely touched. Everything looks injected with artificial colors and chemicals. Gray mashed potatoes. Pink ham. Gloppy vegetable. Hard to tell if it's spinach or broccoli.

A red plastic bottle stands on the dinner tray beside the juice glass. The brand name on the bottle is PEE-buddy.

Under the name is a picture of a winking elf.

The day is catching up on me. I'm aching from last night's grapes. From my twenty-foot fall. From too little sleep. From dragging my sorry ass across the snowdrifts.

And now the ripe surrealness of the Delphi—ancient oracle Agnes and globe-eyed David O. H. Cosgrove II.

I'm not sure I can handle any more. The wrong word. The wrong smell. The wrong thought.

I've got Gupti at my front. Birdwell at my back. Mimi at both sides.

Everybody wants something from me.

Till now, I could handle it. After all, I made it through

everything with Telly. But now my brother is reduced to sticky gray dust and tiny bone shards. Sprinkled in his favorite places: Lincoln Park, Alki Beach, Longfellow Creek, Schmitz Park, the West Seattle Junction. A pinch on the back seat of the No. 22 bus. A teaspoonful at Easy Street Records.

What's left of Telemachus—about a cupful of dust—rests in a little black box in his closet. Above his yellow T-shirts. Beside his stack of guitar magazines.

After Telly, I thought I could handle anything. Now I know there's a limit. I can't handle the sight of PEE-buddy on the dinner tray. Standing next to the plastic-looking ham. And watery spinach. Or whatever it is.

That little elf winking at me.

I stand up. Say, "Find yourself another writer."

Then I'm gone. Racing down the corridor, looking for the nearest exit. Dreadlock glances up from behind the reception counter.

She senses me leaving forever. And I am. I'll never come back. Not to this place, where death and spinach and piss sit side by side on your dinner tray.

chapter 8

By the time I get home, I'm so disgusted, wound up, wiped out, and starving that I wolf down three bowls of Special K, heavy on the C&H pure cane sugar from Hawaii—my "partner in baking for over ninety-nine years."

In my room, I catch a few minutes of *Seinfeld,* but I've seen this one—Kramer and the fire truck—at least five times. So I hop in bed with Charles Bukowski. For weeks, his poems have been stunning me. He slops dirty varnish on the world, and when it dries, you can say only one thing: "Damn!"

I should be studying for my French Revolution test, but I just can't, not with Bukowski lying on the floor.

I set my alarm for 3:30 a.m. and tell myself I *will* study. I place my history book beside my pillow.

Then I fall into Bukowski:

> *Invent yourself and then reinvent yourself,*
> *change your tone and shape so often that they can*
> *never*
> *categorize you.*

Yeah, exactly. This is why I'm a Greek among Romans, a gut talker in a sea of slam hoppers. Hop and Slam, there's so much ranting and flying spit. Everybody's standing on the same street corner making the same damn noise.

Me, I wander alone.

I'm the guy you see standing on the bridge as you flit across in your BMW.

I write my name in water.

When in Rome, do as the Greeks.

When in West Seattle, do as the Aleuts.

Be unto yourself.

Most people trying to write poetry don't get it. They build on fuzzy ideas like anarchy or love. But that's like throwing a punch at the wind. You can't connect. You have to build your poem on images, and tilt those images at your own angle. If you're lucky, they'll come alive. Take two images:

Girl falls asleep on a Greyhound bus.

The moon rises.

By itself, the moon rising is nothing. It's a cliché. But the girl falling asleep and missing the moonrise is everything. It blasts the poem with pain and possibilities. Figure out what those possibilities are and you've got a poem. That's the secret—to close your hand on jagged glass, then open it and find a butterfly.

Bukowski knows this a million times better than I do. A dozen butterflies leap out of his hand whenever he closes it on jagged glass.

God bless you, Uncle Buk.

Pretty soon, my eyelids droop.

Finally—*bam!*—I'm down.

Then Mimi comes home. Slams the door. Giggles. A deep voice follows her into the kitchen.

My eyes pop open.

Mimi's laying the flypaper, priming the spring on the iron jaws.

Telly and I used to joke about it. How guys see only the Indy 500 curves and tight ass. See the face, which makes you smile when you don't know her. It's not a beautiful face, but a face you see from a great distance, very focused.

All my life, men have been peering around freezer doors at Mimi. Pizza-grabbing men. Six-pack-grabbing men. Telly used to grumble: "Don't look at her ass; check out her eyes."

He was right. There is speckled madness in Mimi's eyes. Darting, long-toothed piranhas. Any sane man looking directly into Mimi's eyes would flee.

Pretty soon they're climbing the stairs, *shh-shh*-ing past my room. Through the crack in the door, I see Mimi leading him by the hand. The door to her room clicks shut.

Then the circus begins. They may as well be piping it through a PA system, because I can hear every clownish yuk and creak and cannon shot and moan and whimper.

In five minutes, the circus is over. Mr. Ringling starts to snore. Mimi curses. Mimi sighs. Mimi sobs.

Then silence.

God knows what she's thinking. In my mind, she is staring at the midnight ceiling, wondering what the hell life is all about. Why it takes so much from you. Which is what I'm wondering, too. We have that much in common. No matter our googolplex differences, we have Telemachus in common.

And the vast, sprawling desert he has left us in.

It sure isn't the first time I've listened to Mimi spank ass. I used to bury my head in a pillow to block out the sounds. Now I welcome them. They help me think. I can see how I might be Mimi's son—I'm half crazy. As a poet, I have to be. But Telemachus? He wasn't crazy. How could he be the son of Mimi?

Golden-haired Telemachus—Achilles on a skateboard, Socrates of the alleys. Always skating and pickin' his guitar, sometimes both at the same time. Always jacking us up, making us feel we could be mayors and rock stars. Even poets.

Telly was sunlight. Blond and blue.

I am darkness. Shades of gray and sepia.

I lie awake pondering life's ironies and mysteries till my alarm goes off at 3:30 a.m. I click on the reading light and try to focus on the French Revolution, but the words have all the bang of a soggy firecracker. I just can't wrap my head around Talleyrand and Marie Antoinette. My mind is a bowl of cold oatmeal. I could sleep for a million years. If only I could.

After a while, I fling the book at the wall, swing around, and grab Ruby Tuesday. I drag my desk chair to the window. I've been working on the intro to the Chili Peppers' "No Chump Love Sucker," but it requires a skeleton-fingered stretch, which I'm not up to at 3:45 a.m. So I ditty around on Green Day's "409 in Your Coffee Maker," a simple, mantra-like tune, and "Maggot Brain" by Funkadelic, just six notes endlessly repeated, with a couple variations. Musical treadmills.

For the next hour, I bounce sleepily from hook to hook, noodling and doodling, finding comfort in repetition.

I doze, slumped on the stool, cradling Ruby. In my dream, day is breaking, birds singing, the sun rising. It's a summer-skateboard morning. Telly is out on his famous long board. Shirtless. His board shorts ride low, anchored by the blue elastic band of his Calvin Klein boxers. His curly blond hair flies behind him.

But when I open my eyes, the sky is frozen. The street is bound in blackness and ice.

I start playing "Here Comes the Sun."

As tunes go, it's a hard one to play. If you can master it—the combined pickin' and strummin', all the runs and contrapuntal stuff—you're pretty good. You can hold your head high among real players. Telly practiced "Here Comes the Sun" a million times, laying it on top of the Beatles until you couldn't hear the difference. At our middle school graduation party, he climbed onto a picnic table and played it to a group of wine-sipping moms, swishing his hair, not afraid to open his eyes and smile, the way I am when I stand in front of a crowd. Those moms jumped up from their picnic blankets. Gave him a standing ovation.

Telly capoed at seven, for that sweet harp sound, but I don't capo at all, because I want the deep notes. I want to bend the dark morning into it. Telly knew all the runs. I barely know any. Just the chords—D, G, A7, with a little split on A7.

It starts to go somewhere, and I give it space and do a slow, laid-back version, streaking it with the blues. Ruby sounds wonderful. Sorrowful. She's leading me by the hand, barefoot through the Canadian wheat fields.

I rasp a few lyrics, give them a whiskey tinge, which I can do because I'm a thousand hours behind on sleep and can still smack up the taste of those grapes. But mostly because I'm thinking "Here Comes the S-O-N" instead of "S-u-n."

I end on an arpeggio upstroke. Let it ring, sweet and doomy. Till it soaks into the walls.

I pat Ruby. Reach to put her back in her rocking chair. Then I notice a shadow leaning in the doorway.

I nearly jump out of my boxers.

"Holy shit!"

He shambles in, a tall, rumpled stranger. No "hello." No "good morning." No "sorry for doing all that circus stuff with your mom."

He nods at Ruby. "You mind?"

I do mind. He's a trespasser—worst kind—but it's so sudden, so early and weary, I just shrug. He lifts Ruby out of her rocking chair and sits on the edge of my bed. "Uh-oh," he says when he sees the extra sound hole.

He tweaks the tuning and reaches for my pick. I hand it to him. Our eyes meet.

"Never heard it played like that before," he says. "You dug into it. Made it your own."

He doesn't say I played great, but still, it feels nice. Nobody ever compliments me on my guitar playing or singing. That's probably because, outside of my thicks, I never play to anybody. In front of an audience, I freeze up. Telly and I would jam for hours, and then he'd go and play to any bus-stop grandma. He'd stroll through the West Seattle Junction strumming his guitar. Not me.

But after he died, something changed. Music started to come easier. For some reason, I got better. Almost overnight. I'm not as good as Telly, not by a long shot. But I'm definitely better.

If you apply the same principles to music that you do to poetry—namely, intestines-dragging-the-ground honesty—you will get better. Play it that way, and you can go far with a few chords.

The stranger's words thaw something. I don't mind his being here so much now.

He sniffs and starts to play a folk ditty. He keeps it quiet, out of respect for the sleeping house. Then he plays some blues. His pinkie wakes up, and it's as if he's tickling Ruby under the arms, because she starts to giggle. He's bending the strings. She's making sounds I've never heard before—raunchy, come-here-and-rub-me sounds. He plays a tappy "Great Balls of Fire," singing in a whispery, peppery voice. Between the verses, he fills in with runs, bending it till Ruby is moaning with glee. It's good to hear her laugh, because I'm always bringing her down. Depressing her.

"Yeah," I say when he sews it up. *"Whew!"*

He reaches down and lifts my hairbrush off the floor. It's an old, tarnished silverback. Holding the brush palm on bristle, silver on strings, he begins to play slide.

"Damn," I say. "DAMN!"

Ruby's changed. She's no longer a pale, brooding poet. She's a tanned, blond winkin' country girl. Swiggling her hips on a porch in West Texas.

"Whoa!" I say.

The stranger smiles. Clamps a hand on the strings. "You got another guitar around here?" he asks.

Telly has three guitars, but nobody's gonna touch them.

I turn and stare out the window. Everything comes crashing down.

He says, "Maybe we could sweeten the morning with a little jam."

"You better go," I say. To rub it in, I say, "You're not the first, you know. And every one of 'em can play guitar."

He chuckles. "Every one?"

"Every one."

He shrugs.

"She's gonna wake up soon," I say. "She'll be in a pissy mood. Trust me, you want to be at least fifty miles away."

He shakes his head. "I'm in no hurry. You gotta have another guitar around here somewhere."

Well, hell. Even more than wanting him to go, I want him to stay. I don't know why, but I do.

I get up and duck across the hall to Telly's room, a journey I've made a million times before except not once in the past eight months. I take a deep breath, hold it, and burst in. Inside, the light is different. It's at least one shade brighter than the rest of the house. His guitars are standing in the corner, same as always. His teal blue Fender electric. His Epiphone Thunderbird bass. His Harmony Sovereign acoustic, which he painted red, white, and blue and sprinkled with multicolored teardrops.

These guitars wait for Telly, like he might rush in and grab one. Guitars are like puppies that way. Forever waiting, forever loyal.

I grab the Harmony, my second-favorite guitar in the world. Telemachus got it on our seventh birthday. Gift from Grandpa, a tall, rangy limping man with a white mustache. Liked to stand on the banks of Longfellow Creek, watching Telly and me fish.

Always fuming at Mimi.

Always twinkling at us.

Telly took to that guitar like a frog to a lily pad. It was the first guitar I ever played, too.

I'm using tunnel vision, not wanting to look at his room. Not wanting to see the pictures on the wall, glimpse the familiar yellow T-shirts hanging in the closet, the stacks of guitar magazines, the autographed Tony Hawk poster above his bed.

Still, I feel his ghost. Feel him here. His energy is so intense, it won't die. In death, he casts a warmer glow than anyone alive.

I'm in and out in five seconds.

"Figured," the man says when I return. He stretches out his hand. "I'm Frank."

"Hey," I say. "Jonathan."

We shake.

"What time you leave for school, Jonathan?"

"Seven ten."

"Plenty of time," he says.

He licks into some E blues. His pinkie starts to dart around again. I chord around him, E to A to B7. This time, instead of singing, he drawls over the music, talks it out, kind of like a poet:

I ain't much to look at,
Gettin' old and kinda thin.
I ain't much to look at,
Gettin' old . . . and lame . . . and deaf . . . and blind . . .
and kinda thin.
But there's plenty of good tunes left
In an old violin.

He drawls on like this, all about sitting in rocking chairs by rivers, winking at lusty girls, and coping with hangovers. He sews it up with a sweet riff. Stitch, stitch, ain't it a bitch.

"Why didn't you sing?" I ask.

"It's talkin' blues, Jonathan. Sometimes you can talk a song better than sing it."

He wiggles his pinkie. "Try using this next time. Pinkie can be a godsend, each little note like a bite of candy—an M&M."

He plays an A chord, and his pinkie dances all around his stationary fingers, adding tinges of blue.

"See what I mean?"

"Yeah."

"Give me something."

Uh-oh. I know bits and pieces of a hundred songs, but right now I'm blank.

"I can't sing."

"Bull," he says. "You sound like a young Tom Waits."

"I don't have any hot licks."

"Forget hot licks."

But I can't forget. I gotta show off. Instead of playing from the gut, I try to play the intro to "Sweet Home Alabama." But I fall into nervous-performance mode. My fingers freeze. It's nothing like my gloomy version of "Here Comes the S-O-N," which flowed naturally, but which, if I'd known Frank was listening, I couldn't've played.

"Whoa!" he says. "Hold up. Let's try this."

He plays the opening licks to something called "God's Little Secret." He makes it easy to follow, and we get into the flow, me playing a four-chord rhythm, key of A, and Frank bending into the lead. He starts singing, and pretty soon I'm backing him up. We fall into a two-part harmony. In the middle of about the forty-seventh

"Ooo eeee, don't forget to pray . . ."

. . . the walls begin to pound. We hear:

"Shaaaaddduuuupppppppppp!"

. . . and freeze midstrum.

Frank grins. "Guess our fan base isn't too big."

"Guess not."

"I'll take that as my exit cue."

He sets Ruby in the rocking chair. Shakes my hand again. "Good to know you, Jonathan. Stay with the music. Don't try to be like others. Do it your way, cuz you got something."

I listen to him tiptoe downstairs, open the front door, close it. From my window, I watch his car, a dented, snow-topped red Subaru, roll down the icy street.

"Bet I never see you again," I say.

Day is creeping in.

Irrelevant as ever.

chapter 9

I take a hot shower, dozing under the cascade of water.
Towel off, dress, and head down to the kitchen. I'm pouring a
bowl of Special K when I notice a brown business card on the
counter:

> Frank Conway
> Musician/Music Instructor
> Piano, Guitar, Drums, Flute
> Blues, Folk, Rock, Reggae

Plus all the contact info.
On the back, in pencil, are two words: "Call me."
Does he mean me or Mimi?
I shrug and pocket the card.
Pretty soon, Mimi drifts down. She's wearing her white silk
dragon kimono. Looking like a hooker from hell. All tangled
curls, pale cheeks, hard mouth. Her eye makeup—which glit-
tered last night—looks like black eyes this morning. Her hands
tremble as she sets up Mr. Coffee. I bow my head and shut up.
I've had years of practice. I go easy crunching my Special K.
"*Gawwwdddd,* you chew like a horse," she says. Then, test-
ing the water: "How did you sleep last night, baby?"
Her back is to me.

"Like a polar bear," I say.

Her shoulders relax.

But I can't leave it at that. I have to open my big mouth. "How did *you* sleep, Mimi?"

She stiffens, gnashes her teeth.

"All you ever do is write your damn poetry and play your damn guitar. Who the hell are *you* to judge *me*?"

"Nobody," I say. "I'm nobody."

She aims a finger. "Whatever Dr. Jacobson tells you to do today, do it! If you drag your sorry little poetic ass, you're headed straight back to your father. Do you hear?"

I lift the cereal bowl to my lips and make a loud slurping noise.

Mimi reaches into her kimono for her cell phone, starts to punch the number.

"Hold up!"

I set the bowl down and meet her eye. "No way am I moving back," I say. "I'll live under a bridge with the trolls and transients before that happens."

She nods. "You and the trolls and transients would get along fine."

Mr. Coffee starts to percolate. Mimi skates her cell phone down the counter, grabs the pot, pours a cup, cuts it with Irish Cream. She's steaming.

I realize my mistake. Never mess with Mimi when she's in a threatening mood.

And there is no bigger threat than my father.

It's impossible that Telly and I are his sons. His neck is too thick. His nose is too big. His brain is too small. The back of his hairy hand is as soft as a spanner wrench. Walt Whitman? Never heard of him.

Mimi shakes a finger at me. "If you miss your meeting with Dr. Jacobson, you're . . ."

Mimi doesn't know how to transform words into sticks of dynamite.

". . . burnt toast."

My cell phone burps.

I grab my backpack and head out to the car, Kyle's brother's ancient Volks. The Volks has been painted so many times, what's left is a grayish-whitish-bird-poopish color—same shade as the moon. Dappled with Bondo putty. It's held together with chewing gum and duct tape. Hole under the accelerator. No second gear.

When I get in, Kyle says, "Ladies and gentlemen, Batman has arrived. He who flies off bridges in snowstorms."

Nick, thumbing his phone in the back seat, says, "Lord of the Skies."

The car smells of wet, shampooed hair and cinnamon Altoids.

"How's my favorite MILF this morning?" Kyle says.

"Dude," I say, shaking my head, "not today."

"Just tell me one thing. Is she wearing that kimono with the fire-breathing dragon on the back?"

"Leave it alone, man," I say.

Kyle says, "In case you forgot, *thick-ism* is about truth, and the truth is, your mom was designed by god—with maybe a little help from Aphrodite and final inspection by Madonna—to be a MILF, a Mother I'd Like to—"

"Fuck off," I say.

"Respect," Nick says. "Purify."

Kyle folds into silence. His whole being is a clash of humility and testosterone. Like a monk with a hard-on.

We ease down the snowy street on bald tires, slide through a few stop signs, which is risky because nobody has a license yet. We gain some traction on Delridge, where they've dumped potash.

Nick taps my shoulder. "Jonathan," he says. "Don't try to fly again, okay?"

I nod.

"Promise?"

"Yeah."

Nick sighs. I feel relieved, too. How can I break a promise to Nick?

Kyle thumbs open the Altoid tin and offers me one.

"What time you meet with Gupti?"

"Fourth period," I say, popping an Altoid.

He whistles. "Man, I'm glad I'm not you."

Nick says, "Just say yes to everything. *Yes, yes, yes, yes, yes.* You'll be okay."

"Fuck, no!" I counter.

When we get to Taft, Nick and I jump out and push the car over the icy speed bump into the parking lot. The bell is ringing.

"Just do what she says," Kyle says. "Don't mess with her mind. Do *not* quote Walt Whitman or do your Yoda thing. Else you're gonna split us up. You want that?"

I shake my head. Hold up my fist. "Thicks forever," I say.

"Damn right."

We bump all around.

• • •

"Well, well, well," Mr. Maestretti says as I slip into physics. "The prodigal son has returned."

I slide into my seat in the back. Peguero leans over: "Dude, you really fall off a bridge?"

"Flew off," I say.

Mr. Maestretti raises his voice. "We've been talking about Avogadro's number, Jonathan. Care to remind us who Mr. Avogadro was and the significance of his number?"

Fortunately, I skimmed the chapter a few days back. I'm vaguely familiar with Avogadro and his faggy number. I raise my voice. Jam it with fake confidence.

"Italian physicist," I say. "Came up with a way of stating the number of molecules in a substance."

Mr. Maestretti toggles his hand. "Actually, a mole of a substance. But close enough."

Whew! I've bought myself some downtime.

Peguero pats my back. Lotus LeClerc, sitting two rows in front, turns and winks at me.

In minutes, the sirens of sleep start dancing. They reach up and grab my eyelids. Those little pixies are heavy. I need all of my powers to keep my eyes open. I stretch, wiggle my toes, doodle, even take notes. Somehow, I get through physics.

Between classes, I duck into the bathroom and soak my head under a faucet, paper-towel it dry. In Spanish III, the sirens tantalize me with glimpses of cleavage and thigh. The boldest puckers her lips. *"Tu tiens dos bonitos ojos, Jonathan."*

Miss Sosa stares at me and twice raps her knuckles on my desk. "What are you grinning about, Jonathan? Wake up!"

Between second and third periods, I run into Kyle in the hall. "Man, you look like hell." He drags me over to his locker, opens it, reaches into the toe of an old Dunk High, pulls out an Atomic Fireball.

"Here, suck on some lava," he says.

I pop the little red sphere of candy. Twelve seconds later, my mouth ignites.

"Hiroshima ain't got nothin' on an Atomic Fireball," Kyle says. "It'll get you through that French Revolution shit."

And it does, barely.

Now it's fourth period. Mrs. Scranton takes me back to Gupti's office. "She'll be here in a minute, Jonathan. Are you okay?"

"Phenomenal."

She looks doubtful. "I heard about your fall."

"Twenty feet," I say.

"Have you seen a doctor?"

"No need. It was only twenty feet."

Mrs. Scranton smiles maternally. Shuts the door. Now I'm alone in Gupti's office.

I drop onto the couch, which is low and seems to stretch forever. The Atomic Fireball has worn off. I yawn, rub my eyes. Get up, scan the office for candy, caffeine—anything to keep me going. But there's nothing. Only a little drum from Kashmir.

I pull back a curtain and peer through a window into the neighboring office.

Clarence P. Tillmann Jr. is sitting at his desk. The shriveled jazz god. Taft band leader. On the wall behind him is a giant blowup of a magazine cover from long ago. It shows Mr. Tillmann as a young man, leaning back to back against another jazz god, Dizzy Gillespie. They are wailing on their trumpets. The headline reads "Young Men With Horns."

Mr. Tillmann glances up, sees me. I fling the curtain closed.

Flop down onto Gupti's couch again.

Here come the dancing sirens. This time they're wearing Victoria's Secret lingerie. They do a little pole dance on the inside of my eyelids. Next they lasso me, hogtie me. Giggle all over me. I fight back, but you can't beat those pixies when you're down.

I sink into Gupti's couch. My face feels born for the cushion.

chapter 10

"Jonathan!"

Gupti is shaking my shoulder.

I moan. "Give me a minute."

"Can you open your eyes?"

"The sirens have glued them shut."

"Sirens?"

I roll off the couch and crank some blind pushups. *Hup hup hup!* After about ten, my heart is pumping. Now I can open my eyes. I do a few more pushups to pump the blood into my brain. This is an important meeting, and I don't want to miss anything.

I stand, dust off my knees, and smile at Gupti. She and Mrs. Scranton look worried.

"Jonathan, are you up to this?" Gupti asks in clipped syllables.

"Hey," I say. "It's fourth period. I'm here. Wide awake."

Gupti nods for Mrs. Scranton to leave.

I deliberately don't sit on the couch but on a hard chair. Gupti pulls up a matching chair, facing me.

She takes a deep breath, lets it out. "You saw my letter?"

"Yeah, I saw it."

"And you're prepared to discuss your strategy for success?"

I shrug.

"Jonathan, this is serious. We're talking about your future. The rest of your life."

"Yeah," I say. "My favorite subject."

"Jonathan, you are one of our brightest stars here at Taft, but you will not be promoted to the twelfth grade if you do not take a radically different approach to school."

"Radically?"

"You know what I mean."

Gupti is wearing a beige pajama outfit, a blue REI down vest, and a ten-foot-long white scarf. She's also wearing fat snow boots. She's six two in sandals, but in snow boots she's six four. She reaches for some papers on her desk.

"Here is an inventory of your missing assignments. Note that it does not stop on page one. And note that it does not stop on page two—"

"Let me guess," I say. "It stops on page three."

She flashes the three pages at me, reads a sampling of my most glaring missing assignments, pauses to let it all sink in.

"Can you do this—make it up?"

I shake my head.

"Jonathan, I am not a hardhearted person. I am a compassionate person. I have sympathy for you, perhaps even empathy. Do you know the difference between sympathy and empathy?"

"It's subtle," I say.

"All right," she says. "I'm going to make you a deal. Listen carefully." She exhales. "Jonathan, you must promise to attend every class and do every assignment between now and the end of the year—"

"Deal!"

Her face darkens. "Let me finish."

She closes her eyes. Finds her vital calming center. Her chi. Opens her eyes.

Here it comes.

"And you must pledge to complete the project Dr. Bramwell has proposed."

I groan. "You mean write that damn book?"

"Yes."

"How'm I gonna do that?"

She smiles. It's a smile that contains all the suffering of India. "How? Through hard work and application, that's how. The school year ends in four and a half months. If you wish to be promoted, wish to graduate on time with your classmates, and not with your classmates' younger siblings, you will get to work. You will apply yourself. You will function on all cylinders. It's called self-actualization, Jonathan. You will actually become the you you are meant to be."

A vent opens. A cloud of gloom pours into my mind.

"But how am I gonna write a book in four and a half months?"

"Jonathan, just write something meaningful. And truthful. And rare. And wonderful. Like you do in your poems. What's the title of your poem about Abraham Lincoln—the one you read at the open house last year?"

" 'Baboonery.' "

"Yes. 'Baboonery.' Can you recite it for me?"

"Unh-uh," I say. "I never memorize my poems."

Which is true. Memorization is a form of imprisonment. I write the poems, then free them. *Poof!*

Gupti goes over to her filing cabinet, riffles through some

papers, finds the poem. She puts on her glasses. Straightens into her poetry-reading posture. Lifts her voice:

"Baboonery
The general wrote his wife,
'Darling, our president is the original gorilla.
A baboon. He knows nothing.
He shames the nation.
Blood flows in rivers
at Shiloh
and Antietam
while this baboon
peels bananas and cackles.'
Today, I stood at the bus stop
waiting for the 22.
Mist rolled down Delridge Avenue.
A current of history.
A river of blood
I shed each day
on my jagged journey
to death.
Before I would follow a general
into battle, I would follow
a baboon up a tree
to sit in the high canopy,
cackle, and peel bananas."

Gupti takes off her glasses. Squinches her mind.

"To me, Jonathan, this says something about how we view history. Both the short view and the long. History teaches us that

General McClellan was full of brass and bluster, while Lincoln was rough-hewn but wise. As you approach this new project, pour yourself into it, just as you poured yourself into this poem."

I stare at her. Speechless.

"Jonathan, if anybody can do this, you can. Do we have a deal?"

I shake my head.

Gupti glares. The monsoons of India darken her eyes.

Nick echoes in my mind—"Just say yes to everything." My head goes from shake to parabola. Then from parabola to nod. I know I'm gonna regret this. But I don't want to lose a whole year, either.

Thickness rules.

"Yeah, sure. Deal. I'll do it."

The storm blows away. The sun bursts over Calcutta. Hare Krishna!

"One last thing," Gupti says.

Uh-oh.

"I'll look with special favor upon your situation, Jonathan, if . . ."

She leans close. Her perfume is a drop of Ganges River, a whiff of buttered popcorn. I stare at the red tilak mark on her forehead.

Gupti smiles a secret smile. "I'm a *huge* Pinky Toe fan."

"A what?"

"Pinky Toe—the band. You know, named after . . ." She points to the toe of her snowbooted foot.

I'm blanking.

"Graduation is Friday, June first," Gupti says. "I'd like you to do a Pinky Toe number for us."

"Do a . . . number? You mean—?"

"I mean sing and play your guitar."

"In front of the whole school?"

"The whole school *community,* Jonathan."

"Whoa!" I say. "Hold up! I don't do that. I'm no rock star."

"Oh, nonsense."

I shake my head. "You got me mixed up with my brother. He was the frontman. I'm the shadow man."

Gupti smiles. "Well, Jonathan, it's time you stepped out of your brother's shadow. Besides, I've heard you read your poems in front of hundreds of people. You seem very much in command."

"Hey, there's a big difference. That's poetry. That's trance."

"Music is also trance, Jonathan. And I've heard you play the guitar and sing."

"No you haven't. You've heard Telly play guitar and sing. People confuse us all the time. It's okay. I forgive you."

Gupti says, "Do you remember the last day of school before Christmas break? A Friday. It was dark—raining hard. Somehow, after the final bell, you and Kyle got into the music room. Broke in, I should say. That's a major violation, Jonathan. A serious breach. I could have punished you both, but I didn't."

"Whoa! You heard that?"

She raises a brow. "I understand, Jonathan. It's all about that guitar, isn't it?"

"That guitar" happens to be a custom-built cherry red Rickenbacker 360-6, made with bubinga wood imported from Africa. The Vedder—Eddie the Great, that is—signed and donated it to Taft in honor of Telemachus. He also donated two of his other guitars: a Martin dreadnought; and an Alvarez Yairi acoustic, with a country-gentleman cutaway.

But the "Ric"—oh my god! It's easily the most valuable instrument in the entire Seattle school district. Maybe in the entire country. Nick checked online. Normally, a custom-built Ric 360-6 runs about five grand. But because The Vedder signed it—and had that little brass plate screwed on—it gained instant immortality. It's gotta be worth ten times that much. He smacked it with fame. Slapped it with legend. You could auction it on eBay for a fortune.

I kid you not.

Gupti's little guitar comment has started a train. I hop aboard. Chug back to that rainy afternoon before Christmas. I'm not missing anything because all Gupti's talking about is ethics and integrity.

So I pull quietly out of the station.

Clickety-clack.

• • •

What's the use of a great guitar if nobody plays it? And by order of the Music Department, nobody can play the Ric 360-6. It's too damn sacred.

But I wanna touch base with Telemachus. It's my first Christmas without him.

Kyle lifts the keys that Mr. Takakawa keeps on a screw behind the fuse box. Unlocks the door to the music room. Then he unlocks the inner sanctum—the door to the instrument room. Now we are standing in a dark jungle of giant basses and hanging bassoons. Saxes and kettledrums. The stringed instruments are stacked in hard black cases.

In the back is a tall, narrow closet. Padlock the size of a coffee mug. Kyle tries all the keys. Gets out his pocketknife. In a minute—*voilà!*

The Ric has been sleeping in a glimmering silver case on the upper shelf. I lift it down, carry it out to the music room. Pop the snaps. Lift Ricky out of his plush black bed where he's been sleeping in silk pajamas, like a prince. Smooth my fingers over the little brass plate:

"For Telemachus: RIP and keep in touch. Eddie Vedder."

Not a nick or a scratch. Virginal.

Just like me.

Ah, Eddie, thanks. You crazy skater-rocker-superstar dude. Even though you're world famous, you're just Eddie. Shaggy skater in flapping flannel. Millionaire in scuffed Doc Martens.

Telly and I first met the great Eddie Vedder at Easy Street Records in the West Seattle Junction. To stay sane between tours, he works the counter. He's got this voice—deeeeeeeeeeep. And he carries a song-writing journal, a little spiral notebook, in his shirt pocket. When he's not busy helping customers, he fades to the end of the counter, makes himself invisible, and jots in his journal. Like a poet.

Just watching him, I knew I needed a little spiral notebook, too. And a nubby pencil. That's when I started carrying them everywhere, after seeing Eddie catching all these ideas and jotting them down before they got away.

Advice to fledgling poets: Always carry a little notebook. And a pencil or pen.

Jot habitually, compulsively—and legibly.

Eddie called us the "Chiaroscuro Twins." *Chiaroscuro* is an Italian word meaning "light and dark." He meant hair and eye color, and maybe, subconsciously, something more.

He lives in a castlelike house banked up against a forest of poison oak and alders, overlooking Puget Sound. Two Halloweens ago, Telly got it in mind to pay him a visit.

Our strategy: sneak past the security guards, go over the wall, knock on the door.

Then—and most important—say the code word:

"Guitar."

Guess who opened the door? Unbuttoned flannel shirt and all.

But The Vedder wasn't happy to see us.

He grumbled about security, especially because of his sleeping kids upstairs.

"Hey, Eddie," Telly said. "Trick or treat."

"Go home," Eddie said.

"We're here on business," Telly said.

Eddie looked ready to slam the door. But then Telly says the code word:

"*Guitar* . . . business."

Telly starts his patter. "Hey, I'm lookin' for a new one. So many to choose from . . . We figured, why not ask the greatest guitar player we know. And so here we are."

Eddie grinds his teeth. Then he waves us in "for one minute—one frickin' minute." We tiptoe upstairs, past the bedrooms of his sleeping kids, to his third-floor music studio. It's all bright light, blond furniture, hanging guitars. A giant framed poster of Bob Dylan. A huge control board. A deep couch. Hard chairs. Music stands.

It's like walking into the private sanctum of a grunge-rock Einstein. His own personal music lab. A place of man comfort and dishevelment.

Eddie points to a wall of guitars.

"My first," he says, lifting down a scratched-up Washburn acoustic.

By now, Telly's eyes are popping. He's drooling. He's seen the gleaming cherry red Rickenbacker 360-6.

"Just arrived yesterday," Eddie says. "Custom-built. I de-signed the F holes myself."

Telly reaches out. Smoothes his hand over the lacquered body. Runs his fingers up the neck. Lingers on the inlaid pearl markers.

"Go ahead," Eddie says. "You'll be the first. I haven't gotten around to playing it yet."

It's like an invitation to dance with Cinderella, and Telly's suddenly bashful. So he shakes his head, grabs a plainer girl, an Alvarez Yairi acoustic. Eddie swaps the Washburn for a Martin D-28 dreadnought. There's a fishbowl full of picks on the cof-fee table and capos scattered about.

They sit on stools, tune up, and start to noodle. I sit on the couch. Guitarless. Unworthy.

In every way, Telly is a better player than me. And a better singer. If I ever had doubts, I know it now. He knows ten times as many chords, and he can pick a lot better. My style is slower, bendier. I'm a sloppy, jacked-down small-town guitar player, a moron's version of Stevie Ray Vaughan. Maybe that's because I don't have Telly's long fingers or technical flash. I hide behind simplicity.

We both know it. We know it now, forever, because I don't pick up a guitar. Don't have the guts. Not in front of The Vedder.

So I sink into the timid couch. But that's okay with me. That's where I belong in the presence of Eddie the Great.

In the course of noodling, Eddie and Telly start to form patterns, and the patterns start to sound familiar. Eddie guides it with glances that say "like this" or "key of G." Telly picks it up right away. Eddie hunches over his dreadnought and slips into a trance. Then he starts singing.

I've heard the Great Vedder a thousand times on CDs, but nothing sounds so raw and achy as the real thing.

His voice is the hammer of Thor and the velvet glove of Jesus rolled into one. And he's not even using a mike.

The song they do is "Masters of War," a chug-a-chug-a rant against the military madness. Against all the boneheaded generals and lip-synching politicians.

Listening to that song, I begin to feel strongly there's only one thing America can do—hold a global peace picnic on the banks of the Mississippi.

Then they do "Society," which is just the opposite, a spare, sweet, wistful song about soul isolation. In the midst of Telly's rhythm, Eddie plays a lead riff, and every note rings purely and humbly, except one, which he bends. And that one bent note haunts the entire song. It is the cry of all humans for love.

On good guitars, freshly strung, you can really make it hum. I wonder about those sleeping kids downstairs, but Eddie's probably soundproofed the studio.

They stitch it up, and Eddie drapes himself wearily over the D-28.

"You got something?" he says to Telly.

This is like asking a bird to sing in the morning.

Telly glances at the Ric. "Hey, if you don't mind . . ."

Eddie shrugs. "Go ahead."

Telly jumps up and swaps guitars. Now he's cradling the Ric. Holding it like a swaddled newborn, with tender awe. He pops in a cable, turns the volume to just louder than acoustic. Clamps a capo way up on seven. Presses the Ric tightly against his hip. Plays an arpeggio D chord. Immediately you hear the Ric's distinctive voice. A ringing softness backed with power. Like Hannibal standing in the Alps and whispering into the valley.

Telly changes to a heavy pick. In front of The Vedder, this takes a full nut sack. When you choose a heavy pick, you're going for a crisp, confident sound. You better hit every note. Because if you trip on the wrong one, it's over. I would've chosen a thin pick, because you can kind of hide your mistakes.

But Telly goes for bold.

He anchors himself.

Waits for god's permission.

Then he bursts into the angel-note intro to "Here Comes the Sun."

It just pours out of him. Bright and shiny.

A perfect sunrise.

A golden dewdrop.

Not a hair nervous, even though this is The Vedder.

EV—Eddie the Great.

Mr. Wes C. Addle.

But now Eddie's just another guy draped over a guitar on a moonless Halloween night.

And the sun is rising. Warming his cheeks.

Telly's voice finds it. He's a better singer when he sings softly. When he shouts, he's only average. But softly, he can go all kinds of places. You believe him when he sings about how long and cold and lonely the winter has been.

He plants himself on D, plays the rundown.

Plays the contrapuntal stuff on the low strings, the upward bass run.

I've never heard him play so well. His fingers spider-dance across the frets.

It's like the Ric knows exactly where to go and is guiding Telly to the summit. He can make no mistakes. None. The Ric won't let him.

Telly sews it up.

Stitch, stitch, ain't it a bitch.

Ching!

The room rings silent on a final, sublime D.

Telly's as stunned as I am. He stares at the Ric in awe. A crazy, saintly smile spreads across his face.

The Vedder remains draped over his dreadnought. Pondering. Everything hangs in the air. Then he cracks a grin.

"Dude," he says. "DUDE! How old are you?"

• • •

That afternoon in the Taft music room, Kyle plugs me in. Not to a baby amp, but to the one used at football games: Fat Phyllis. She has a slightly smaller twin: Big Bertha. These two amps are the size of Ford and Toyota pickups. Kyle leaves Bertha parked on the sidelines, thank god.

I tune up and lick into the intro to "All Apologies," a Kurt Cobain power riff. *Whoa!* Even at five percent volume, it's gigantic. A magnitude-twelve earthquake. Kyle shudders gleefully.

"Naw, man," I say. "Bring it down."

Kyle tweaks down the volume, then plants a mike in front of me.

"Play 'Desecration Smile,'" he says.

I open with a C-sharp minor chord because I can't handle John Frusciante's four-fret stretch. I do, however, play his added ninth on E, which is like putting a dash of paprika on your poached eggs. I play the tune crunchy but gentle. Sing it whispery, hoping nobody will hear.

Kyle grabs Mr. Takakawa's cowboy hat off a hook, dips it low over his eyes, and joins me for the chorus, banging bongo-style on a drum case.

The strings of the Ric are silken. I mess up a couple times, but the Ric is so sweet, so forgiving, it covers my mistakes.

Any guitar that's smarter than you is a work of art.

The Ric is Michelangelo's *David.*

• • •

"You heard that?" I ask Gupti when she wraps up her lecture on the principles of student discipline, as inspired by Shiva and Vishnu.

"Oh, dear boy," she says. "I heard every last note. You were . . . how can I say it? Fabuloso."

"Fabuloso?"

"You know, Jonathan," Gupti says, "talent is like the grape on the vine. It sweetens only when we nurture it, let the sun shine upon it. But it shrivels if we keep it in the dark. You must share your many gifts."

"Yeah," I say. "I don't want them to turn into raisins."

Gupti smacks my knee. "I have full confidence in you, Jonathan. Let's seal our agreement with a handshake."

"Why not."

We shake. Her hand is trucker size.

"Good," Gupti says. "Now our strategy for success is in place. Doesn't that feel better?"

She stands, flips her scarf over her shoulder. "Off to class with you."

I slump out of the chair and reach for the doorknob.

"Oh, Jonathan."

"Yeah?"

Gupti smiles. "If you really want to please me, you'll do my all-time favorite Pinky Toe number, 'Crossing the River Styx.' Will you do that for me?"

I've never heard of the tune. But in ignorance, all seems equal.

"Why not."

"Fabuloso," she says.

As I step through the door, I whisper:

"Fabuloso."

chapter 11

Next is lunch, but my only appetite is for sleep. In the hall, I catch the eye of José the janitor. He's all brushy mustache and coveralls.

"Amigo," he says, shaking his head. "You look like a zombie from hell."

I grab his arm. "Dude, you gotta let me catch a nap in the furnace room."

"Sure, amigo, sure."

"Gracias, gracias."

Tucked behind the furnace, in a narrow little nook fanned by industrial hum and chuff, on the warm concrete floor, I fall instantly, dreamlessly asleep. Forty-five minutes later, in the middle of the bell, José jabs me with a broom handle, sweeps the dust off my ass.

I've filled my tank about two percent, but it's enough. José looks tragic. *"Amigo, amigo,"* he says.

We bump fists sadly. "You saved my life, José. *Usted guardó mi vida."*

"Always do, Jonathan. You and Telly. *Yo lo adore."*

"Yeah," I say. "He loves you, too."

"Con dios, amigo."

"Con dios, man."

I have just enough gas to get through chemistry. Last period is study hall, and I don't feel I'm violating my agreement with Gupti by ditching it.

I hop the northbound 128. The snow has melted a bit, then refrozen, then melted a bit more. California Avenue is a deep, slushy soup. The sky is a dirty gym sock. The world is no longer a perfect virgin, but a toothless slut in rags.

From the bus stop, I trudge the last quarter mile to the Delphi. I stop on the bridge over Schmitz Park. Gaze at the noisy creek hidden under a pillowy bed of snow. It's forty or fifty feet down. I could lie there forever.

I push into the Delphi and once again inhale the B.O. of death. Inhale the deodorizing lemon spritz that tries to hide it. Hear the game-show laughing in the lounge. See the cancer-perforated guests sitting on couches or watching from wheelchairs. The TV laughs and laughs.

If there is a hell, it is here.

I sit down in the lobby. Fish out my notebook and pencil. Sink into the chair. Scrawl:

Chaos XV
All year, I've been
building fences
on the ragged
boundary of death.
Just when I'm ready
to wipe my hands and slouch away,
I open the gate,
step in.
Shove it closed behind me
(good ranch hand that I am).

*Yippee-aye-oh-cuy-ay!
I'm back in
Death County, USA.*

Poems are best when you stir in light and dark, plant ironies under paper cups, like firecrackers.

Walking down the Delphi corridor, I feel the blood of Telly rise in me.

Twin blood. More powerful than ordinary brother blood.

That night is an old movie, remembered in flickering images. Telly counting crumpled one-dollar bills. Stuffing them into a Ziploc bag. Grabs his long board. Skates off. It's just past 11:30 p.m. on April 17. Typical misty-slick Seattle night. He's wearing his flip-flops, blue board shorts, Seahawks hoodie.

Walgreens is six blocks away.

"Back in twenty. E-Z."

Famous last words.

But his final last words were these . . .

"Adios, dude."

• • •

Today, a new girl sits behind the reception counter at the Delphi. Like Dreadlock, she has weird hair. Must be a job requirement. Day-Glo blue. Bowl cut. Big glasses. Black rims.

She locks me in her sights. *Blam!*

"Coward!" she says, jumping out of her chair. "Why did you run away?"

It's Dreadlock. She's cut her hair. Straightened it. And no more wheelchair.

"Guess they cured your polio," I say.

"Nobody gets polio anymore. God, what a coward!"

Whoa!

I check her out, something I didn't do while she was in the wheelchair, out of respect. She's average height, maybe an inch shorter. Thin and tight, like a swimmer. Small breasts. Behind those glasses, almond eyes. God knows if she's Ethiopian or banshee. Her skin—not a zit. Must be mixing some kind of exfoliator with sea salt. But she's a shade too pale, especially around the eyes. Maybe too much midnight reading, like me.

Nose, neck, jawbone—the royal line. Her mouth, like a diamond, is a ten on the hardness scale.

She jerks her head. "C'mon."

I follow her down the corridor. Passing room 101, I glimpse David Cosgrove sitting in his wheelchair, watching TV. Then I remember: he doesn't watch, he listens.

Dreadlock stops at room 114—Agnes's room. It's dim inside. The little waterfall gurgles in the corner. The standing fan breezes back and forth. I gotta hand it to the decorator; it's like we just stepped from a Costco aisle onto Waikiki Beach. All we need is ukulele music.

Agnes is watching a soap opera. A man lies comatose in a hospital bed. A curvy blonde sobs over him. The blonde is overacting, throwing her arms everywhere. Even the comatose man is overacting.

Agnes looks as ancient as a Dead Sea Scroll. Her hair is whiter than her pillow.

Dreadlock says, "You were right. He's back."

Agnes looks up from the soap. Her expression transforms into a glow. She reaches for my hand. Her clasp is fragile, as if a hard squeeze by me might break her bones. She strokes my hand, grandma style.

"Take the road down to the sea," she says.

I glance at Dreadlock, who holds a finger to her lips.

"Free the swimmers," Agnes says. "They've been under so long. Show them the way."

"What *is* the way?" I ask.

Agnes lets go of my hand and pokes my chest.

"You know," she says. "Where's your lute?"

"My lute?"

Dreadlock says, "You were supposed to bring a lute, remember?"

"Hey, who do you think I am, Romeo? Nobody's had a lute for five hundred years."

"Well, next time bring one," Dreadlock says. She turns to Agnes. "He promises he'll bring a lute next time. And he'll play for you. Right, Jonathan?"

"Yeah, why not."

Agnes says, "I'm ninety-nine years old."

Dreadlock beams. "That's wonderful, Agnes."

"I want to be an angel."

Dreadlock rubs her arm. "You will be, Agnes."

"Float a turd," Agnes says.

Ah, there it is again.

Jagged glass and butterfly.

No doubt about it, Agnes is a poet.

• • •

I rap on David Cosgrove's door. Slip inside.

David sniffs. "Is that you, Jonathan?"

"Yeah, it's me."

His skin looks yellow today. Like the anchor on CNN. He reaches for the remote and clicks off the TV.

"Anything you want to get off your chest?"

"Not really."

"Anything you want to ask me?"

"You really blind?"

"Black dungeon blind."

"How? I mean . . ."

"Severe, chronic macular degeneration," he says, "to the umpteenth degree."

"Whoa!"

"Bad genes, Jonathan. Fortunately, they hibernated for the first seventy years and I could see fine."

"What else is wrong?"

He chuckles. "Let's take an inventory. I have the Big C—cancer, or more precisely, aggressive mantle cell lymphoma. I have a weak ticker, or more precisely, congestive heart disease. I got a new hip last year and barely survived the surgery. Now I've got a state-of-the art fake hip, just no strength to use it. I have a prostate the size of Texas. I take some fifty pills a day and am hooked on half of them. They make me pee a lot. Those are the larger brush strokes. If you're into pointillism, I'll give you the smaller ones some other time."

"Jeezus."

"Amen, brother."

"Just being blind—that must suck."

"Blindness is the least of my worries, Jonathan. Everyone should experience being blind, if only for a few days. The world can be filled with garish light."

Garish light. I slip out my notebook and jot this down.

"It can be a terribly empty place, Jonathan."

"You got that right."

"Let's try something. Turn out the lights."

I hit the switch. The room goes dark.

"And close the shades."

I lower the shades, twist them tight. Now it's dark—nearly black dungeon dark. The only light is the crack under the door and an orange glow in the light switch. I can't see David Cosgrove, other than as a black blob. The clock begins to tick loudly.

"Right now, we're both blind," he says. "In darkness, everything is different. Time. Place. Tone."

"Tone?"

"Yes, especially tone," David says. "The world is quieter, not so frantic. Your imagination awakens and begins to fill the canvas. You come to see that blindness is not a locked door but a different door. Remember, I could see fine for the first seventy years of my life, so I have an encyclopedia of memories to draw from, all bathed in light."

"But you can't even see to take a piss," I say. "You can't see that it's snowing outside."

"Is it snowing outside?"

"No. But during the storm—"

"I saw it all, Jonathan. The inner eye. A word or two of description from the staff. Oh yes, the storm was very real to me."

"Look," I say, "one thing you gotta know about me: I always tell the truth."

"Of course," David says. "I want you to be truthful with me."

"Well, the truth is, I hate this place."

"I hate it, too, Jonathan."

"I'll just say it now, man. I pity you."

"Why? Because I'm old and sick?"

"No, because you try to put a happy face on stuff, like being blind."

"Not always happy, Jonathan. Some memories are unhappy. One most of all. Do you have any memories that trouble you?"

"Put it this way," I say. "Not a day goes by that I don't think about jumping off a bridge."

David says, "I've stood on that bridge myself."

"If I was you, I'd get in my wheelchair and roll out the door and just keep on going. Even if I was blind."

"Where would you go?"

"I'd get on the first bus—the fifty-one or fifty-five or one-twenty-eight—and ride it all the way to the end of the line. They got those things for wheelchairs, you know."

"Suppose I board that bus, Jonathan. Where do I go when I reach the end of the line?"

"Just ride the bus all day. Transfer. Hop the 'Night Owl.' I don't care. Anywhere beats this place."

"Feeling it now?"

"Feeling what?"

"Your blindness."

"Dude, all I feel is sleepy. I haven't had a good night's sleep in months."

"Why is that, Jonathan?"

"Dragons."

"Ahh," David says. "Let's make this our first rule: absolute honesty. There's a fresh pillow around here somewhere. And that recliner is very comfortable. Catch yourself forty winks. I'll guard against those dragons."

"No thanks."

This throws him. I sense he's used to being in control. Well, that ain't gonna happen with me.

"How old are you, Jonathan?"

"Almost seventeen. How old are you, David?"

"Almost eighty-eight."

"Pretty damn young," I say, "compared to Agnes."

"Yes, I'm a spry youth compared to her."

"She's crazy."

"We're all a little crazy, Jonathan. If we weren't, life would be pretty dull."

"All she talks about are lutes and dark swimmers."

"Yes," David says. "I've heard about those dark swimmers."

"But, hey, dementia might be kind of cool. You wouldn't have to remember."

"True," David says. "What are you remembering now?"

"Well, since we're being absolutely honest, man, I'm remembering how much I don't wanna be here. Because you're nothing but a sick, blind old man."

My words stab.

"Sick, yes," he says, finally. "Old, yes. But no more blind than you, Jonathan."

I flip the switch. The light bombs me. David Cosgrove doesn't blink. His eyes don't even pinpoint. He sits gnarled and cancer-tanned in his wheelchair.

I stand. "Been nice knowing ya, dude."

"Jonathan, I'd like to offer you a job."

"Hey, you don't get it. I don't wanna be here."

"I think you need to be here, Jonathan."

"Oh yeah? And why do you think that?"

He taps his head. "Old man's intuition."

He points to a door in the corner of the room.

"Inside that closet, you'll find a suitcase. I want you to take it home with you."

I open the door to the closet. Inside are some hanging pajamas, a faded Mariners ball cap, fresh towels. In the back is an old leather suitcase. Scratched and scarred. It's blazed with the stickered glory of old travels: the Maldives, Patagonia, Wake Island, Tahiti. Nobody has suitcases like this anymore. It's right out of an old movie starring Humphrey Bogart. I grab the leather handle and lift. Jeezus, it's gotta weigh seventy-five pounds.

"Study everything inside," David says. "If you have questions about how we operate around here, ask Katie."

"Katie?"

"Your new friend."

"You mean—?"

"From now on, we'll meet twice a week, every Wednesday and Sunday afternoon. That will give me time to rally my memory. Charge my batteries. Now I'm tired. I must ask you to leave."

His hands fumble for PEE-buddy on the bedside table. The bottle elf winks at me.

I drag the suitcase into the corridor. Shut the door.

Damn! What am I doing? I don't even want this job.

And I forgot to ask about pay. Now I'm hauling a heavy suitcase, with not a penny to show for it. Once again, I've been exploited.

Passing the reception counter, I snap my fingers at Dreadlock.

"Live short," I say. "Die young."

She glances at the suitcase. Gives me a pirate smile. Glinting cutlass.

"Next time bring your lute, Jonathan!"

"Adios, *Katie!*"

chapter 12

I hop a southbound 128. At the Junction, I lug the suitcase into 7-Eleven and buy a four-pack of Red Bull and a bottle of NoDoz. Maximum strength. Waiting for the No. 22, I pop three NoDoz and guzzle a Bull.

By the time I get home, the caffeine and taurine are kicking in. A hole is forming in the dark circus tent of my mind. I see patches of blue.

In my room, I make a stack of all my schoolbooks. Tell myself I'll spend half an hour on each subject. That'll cover a lot of ground fast. I'm a good skimmer.

David Cosgrove's suitcase stands on my floor, on a pile of dirty clothes. I study it. One sticker says MURCHISON FALLS, UGANDA.

"Murchison," I mumble.

I grab Ruby Tuesday. Strum a ditty:

Hey, Murchison, how'm I gonna do it?
Get it all done?
Hey, Murchison,
How'm I gonna get the battle won?

Then I remember another ditty. Something I've been messing with for a few weeks. I reach into my pick jar and grab a light one.

The ditty starts high on the tenth and twelfth frets, then hops down, two or three frets at a time. Then I plant a simple A chord, which sounds really nice juxtaposed with everything else. Then an E chord, because they work well together. Stitch it with a bass run—E, F#, G.

My pickin' becomes a strum, something a little funky, which I semi-mute with the butt of my palm. Then I play a haunting chord—I think it's an F#7—and balance it with a punkie chord, god knows what that is. But those two chords are like poetry. Side by side, they clash perfectly. Jagged glass and butterfly. Light and dark. Chiaroscuro.

For a ringing moment, the whole world stands on the arched bridge between F#7 and that mystery chord.

It's a good tune, all my own. Captures Telly, his sweetness and complexity. A strawberry dipped in balsamic vinegar.

Pretty soon a half hour's past. The stack of schoolbooks stares at me.

"Two minutes," I say.

I fire up my laptop. While waiting to log on, I pop another Red Bull and glug it down. Ahh, sweet taurine.

But while the taurine is cleansing my mind, the glucose and sucrose are making my teeth ache.

On YouTube, I google Gupti's band, Pinky Toe, plus the song "Crossing the River Styx," and find pages and pages of versions, some by Pinky Toe, but others by a circus of characters: a sexy pole dancer, a ten-year-old piano virtuoso, the cartoon character Eric Cartman of *South Park,* even the Michigan Marching Band.

I click on the image of Pinky Toe performing "Crossing the River Styx" at a concert in Englewood, New Jersey.

Fade to the keyboard player. He's an old rocker with—*gulp!* Is that a toupee? Jeezus, he's gotta be sixty. His sweaty forehead shimmers under the stage lights. He sings in an almost-falsetto:

I'm crossing the River Styx.
From Charon I wrest the oar,
To speed my soul to the Plutonian Shore.

I lean close. Nose right up to the screen.

'Cause I've got to be free,
To lie upon the breast of Persephone
In the land of Nevermore . . .

Slowly, I push myself back.

When he zips it up—tickles the final ivories, turns his expensively tanned, fashionably aged rock 'n' roll forehead to the camera to shimmer one last time—I notice that I've crushed the Red Bull can. Now it's a flat metal cookie. Sweating inside my palm.

Congratulations, Pinky Toe! You have single-handedly written and performed the PUSSIEST song in music history.

It's not that "Crossing the River Styx" sucks a thousand percent. It's sort of catchy, in a sugary way.

But it's fake. Untrue. Unlived.

Words scrawled on paper, set to music, with no bleeding to back them up.

You can't make up pain. It has to be real.

There's no way I can do this song.

Not in front of the whole frickin' school *community.*

Sorry, Gupti.

Cross the River Styx with somebody else.

I'd rather flunk. Graduate with Nick's little brother in ten years.

My schoolbooks stare up at me from the floor. I grab *Integrated Math* and fling it at the wall. Look for the ding, find a dent shaped like a crescent moon.

One by one, I fling my books:

Main Currents in Physics—bang!

Through the Eyes of Monsieur Talleyrand—bang!

Spanish III—bang!

Last is Birdwell's text—*The Art of Poetry and Fiction.* I rip off both covers and pitch it. A burning fastball.

Bulked on steroids.

Strike three!

This leaves just me and Murchison.

David Cosgrove's suitcase is too big to throw against the wall. So I kick it. It topples over. Damn if both the latches don't spring open.

I tuck my toe under the top and flip it back.

Now I see why the suitcase is so heavy. It's stuffed with framed pictures, photo albums, bundled letters, notebooks, journals. All tinged yellowish or brownish with age.

At the bottom is a dark suit of clothes. A uniform. The sleeves have two gold stripes. Brass buttons, tarnished. A squashed officer's hat.

The odor of musty mothballs and ancient wool fills my nostrils.

I've opened a door in time. Back when old people were young. And light was different—more innocent and sorrowful.

One framed picture is of a young dude in a Navy uniform. Same two stripes. I wonder if it's David O. H. Cosgrove II, but the face is so bland it's hard to tell.

I page through a photo album. Picture after picture of Navy scenes.

Sailors in white uniforms lining the deck.

Sailors standing beside big antiaircraft guns.

Sailors playing softball under palm trees. Wearing T-shirts and dog tags.

Plus battle pictures. Pinpoints in the sky that must be enemy planes. Puffs of smoke. Sinking ships.

I study the captions:

"Pearl Harbor, 4 Jan. 1942. The day I board the *Gabriel Trask*."

"Coral Sea, 7 May 1942. The *Lexington* has been mortally wounded. We threw down nets and hauled in eighty-two men. Many badly burned. Lost seven in the first hour."

"Santa Cruz Islands, 26 Oct. 1942. Antiaircraft shells fill the sky above the *Enterprise*. She lives to fight another day, but the *Hornet* didn't make it. We can't afford to lose any more carriers."

"En route to Wellington, NZ, 29 Nov. 1943. Looking forward to first shore leave in six months."

And so on.

I drag the suitcase over to my bed. Pull the light closer.

Then I grab a stack of photo albums. The paper is brittle. I flip carefully.

After a few pages, I reach for another Red Bull. I've got

the whole night ahead of me. Just need to fuel myself with taurine.

I can do my homework later. Like around four a.m.

I'll write after that.

But first I want to hang out with Murchison. Take a little trip back in time.

To Pearl Harbor.

And the Coral Sea.

chapter 13

It's Wednesday morning. Between NoDoz and Red Bull, I'm getting close to my no-sleep record. Not counting catnaps and glazed trances, I've been awake for three days and nights.

And I'm not even sleepy. Just the opposite—I'm buzzed.

Brain firing on all cylinders.

I wrote a poem last night, "Image of the Sea."

That just warmed me up for the two hours I spent polishing "Tales of Telemachus." Writing is the best feeling, except for sex, which I've never had. Except with myself. I practice for the big day practically every day.

I've practiced four thousand three hundred and twelve times.

I practiced at four a.m. this morning. Reading about the French Revolution got me thinking about Marie Antoinette, who got me thinking about Lotus LeClerc, who sits two seats ahead in Mr. Maestretti's class. That got me thinking about Lotus's mom, who picks her up in a Dodge Durango, who wears gypsy skirts and has a very nice ass.

Perfect blend of tight and jiggly.

I used to be a breast man, but I'm becoming an ass man.

They say, as you get older, you become an ass man. It's a higher form of evolution.

If so, I have somehow evolved without ever sampling a single breast.

Or ass.

When taurine meets testosterone, and you add artificial flavors, you think these thoughts.

I thought about Dreadlock, too. But I pushed her away and focused on Lotus's mom's gypsy ass.

That's all it took.

Later, I skimmed my homework and pumped in the minimum amount of knowledge I need to stay afloat. To uphold my bargain with Gupti.

As for Pinky Toe . . .

Hopeless.

• • •

Down in the kitchen, I build a bowl of Special K in the image of Mount Rainier. But it starts looking more like a milk-engorged breast. I slice a bruised banana on top, for the potassium.

Cap it with C&H Pure Cane Sugar from Hawaii.

I wolf the cereal, and as I'm slurping the dregs, my phone burps. Kyle has arrived.

I scoop up my backpack. Then I shoulder Ruby Tuesday. Been a long time since I've packed her up.

Today, she's traveling.

Yippee-aye-oh-cuy-ay.

When I open the door to the Volks, Kyle says, "Why the guitar?"

"Ain't no guitar, man. It's a lute."

I jam Ruby in back with Nick, who's busy texting and doesn't bother to look.

Kyle says, "What the hell's a lute?"

Nick says, "Medieval stringed instrument."

Kyle says, "Mid-*evil?*"

Nick says, "Court guys played them for Henry the Eighth."

I say, "Court guys in pointy, turned-up shoes."

"Oh, yeah," Kyle says knowingly. "I think they played some lutes in *Braveheart.*"

Through the hole under the gas pedal, the world is a slushy gray blur. The Volks's engine grinds deafeningly.

Kyle is eyeing me weirdly again. "Man," he says, "you sleep in a coffin last night?"

"Didn't sleep."

"How come?"

"Too busy discovering stuff about myself."

"Like what stuff?"

"Sleep gets in the way."

"Of what?"

"Everything—art, life, truth."

Kyle shakes his head. "Another day in paradise, dude."

The bell is ringing as we pull into the lot. Nick and I tumble out and push the Volks over the speed bump.

Then I suck it up and face the day purely, which means I either doze or swagger through all of my classes.

But I'm there.

Only eighty-two more days of this.

Thank you, Gupti. Thank you very much.

chapter 14

Normally, I don't show myself in public with a guitar. It's so cliché. Every seventh grader and junior popcorn salesman struts around West Seattle with a guitar on his shoulder, thinking he's Jimi Hendrix Jr.

But today, Ruby is a lute. So I don't mind toting her onto the bus.

Soon I'm wandering down the corridor of the Delphi. Swimming through that Sargasso Sea, where death lurks below, nibbling your toes.

But something's different today.

Dreadlock is sitting behind her counter, as usual. Her hair isn't dready or clowny, but long and straight. Beyoncé brown. She looks half girl next door, half pop princess.

Because she's wearing glasses, she also looks half sexy librarian.

The look is jarringly pleasant. But I try not to stare. Because I figure that's the point.

Still, I'm thinking, *Show us your real hair. Don't be fake. Fakery is the path to soul desolation.*

The residents in the TV lounge pay no attention to me. And they pay no attention to Drew Carey jabbering on *The Price Is Right*.

Because today the price isn't right.

Just ask Death. He's walking down the corridor, a gorilla-shaped guy pushing a stainless steel gurney.

Rolling closer and closer.

Everybody senses him. They hold their heads at a funny angle.

On the gurney is a human being. Once alive.

Now in a gray zippered bag.

The centrifugal force of this fact slams me against the wall. I'm suddenly cold. I can't move.

Death rolls closer. At the reception island, he turns and takes the side exit into the parking lot. He struggles with the door.

Dreadlock rushes over and holds the door for Death. She goes outside with him and the gray zippered bag on the gurney. When the door shuts, the centrifugal force is neutralized. I take a deep breath and follow them outside.

Death is opening the back of a van. In the gray light of day, he's smaller. Less imposing. His hair is orange. His face is freckled pink.

He runs the gurney at the fender and the whole thing collapses, slides neatly inside. Like ramming a grocery cart into its home chain.

The former human being inside the gray zippered bag is now resting comfortably inside the van.

Death shuts the doors. Wipes his hands on his hips. Lights a cigarette. He's a Marlboro man.

"Thanks, Katie."

"Thanks, Gary."

Death gets in and drives off.

"Anybody I know?"

She kicks the slush. Shakes her head.

"What's that?" she says, pointing to Ruby.

"It's a lute," I say.

She smiles, sadly.

• • •

The TV is flickering silently in Agnes's room. Dreadlock draws the shades closed. She pushes a button, and the hospital bed raises Agnes to an upright position.

"Well, Agnes, he finally brought his lute," Dreadlock says. "Just like you prophesied."

Agnes comes into focus. Beams at me. "Float a turd," she says.

Ahhh!

This statement is so irrelevant that it crosses some invisible line and achieves relevance, in a poetic way.

"Same to you, Agnes."

Dreadlock takes a brush from the side table and runs it through Agnes's hair. The old woman sighs sumptuously. For an instant, I see who she might've been. Just erase a million wrinkles. Add a few teeth. Turn that hair dark. Tap her with a wand.

Eighty-five years ago, some long-dead farm boy hiding behind a tree in some apple orchard must've drooled over her.

Time ravages, but it doesn't totally hide. Not if you look closely.

Agnes rolls her hands. "Play—play!"

I unzip the gig bag. Slide bashful Ruby into my arms. Ruby the Lute. I fish a pair of old shades from the zippered pouch. Put them on. (This is a public performance, and I need to hide behind something.) I dig out some picks, choose a thin one for the thinner sound, which is probably closer to the sound a lute would make.

I slide to the floor, back against the wall.

Fast-tune on the fifth fret. Pluck some chimes.

Then I cradle my medieval beauty. Summon up images of Henry VIII and Mel Gibson in a kilt.

Hmmm.

What do you play to a ninety-nine-year-old woman who thinks your guitar is a lute? Who talks about dark swimmers? Who wants to be an angel?

Definitely not "Californication."

And I don't know any Barry Manilow.

Only one tune I know seems to fit, an ancient rock-poetry number with oracle-like overtones called "Knight Flight."

The secret is in the strum. Two beats. Half beat. Five beats. Half beat. Three beats.

I find it. Chord it. C to E minor . . . C to E minor.

Hammer a bass line.

I play this over and over, building a mood somewhere between outer space and King Henry VIII's court. Somehow, this surreal intersection seems appropriate for the Oracle at the Delphi.

Now I'm practically in a trance. I open my mouth, add a bit of synthesizer to my voice:

"Tell the lords the King is dead.
The astronauts have gone to bed . . ."

I peek at Agnes and Dreadlock. They stare saucer-eyed at me. I have no idea how I sound to them, but I sound okay to myself. Maybe Jimmy Crockett, who wrote the tune, would have problems with my arrangement, but I don't.

Agnes jerks. She sits straight up. Before I can get to the part about the multiple vitamins and god's love, she starts singing along with me. Actually, she's a beat behind, so she comes across as an echo.

"Tell the lords the King is dead.
The astronauts have gone to bed . . ."

She starts to sway, swinging on the lutey vine between C and E minor.

And then she snatches the song away from me. Begins to chant her own lines. Her voice turns whispery. What comes out is part poetry. Part dirge. Part oracle. Part drivel.

Down in the sea the swimmers drown,
Shackled in darkness, all around.
Waters rise; I hear their cries.
Free the swimmers in the dark.
Free the swimmers in the dark.

Over and over. Chanting:

Free the swimmers in the dark.
Free the swimmers in the dark.

All spiced with insanity.
Prophecy.
Enlightenment.

Demented gobbledygook.

In all my thousands of guitar-hunkered hours, this moment is the weirdest. I have no idea where Agnes is coming from, what well she drinks from. But her song is pure. Unfaked.

It's exactly the kind of music I like to make.

Reaching for the unknown. The painful and urgent.

The tune could get boring fast, so I toss in little chord jams—C to F to G to A. Plus a seventh here, a ninth there.

Agnes sways.

After about ten minutes of this, she is sweating. The twinkle in her eye fades. She falls back on her pillow.

Dreadlock has been holding her hand. Now she pets the ancient, cotton head.

Lowers the bed. Pulls the blanket up. Tucks her in.

"Go to sleep, Agnes."

"Dear ones," Agnes mumbles. "Dear ones."

I play a final, quiet jam. Plant a penultimate A. Stitch it with a hungry D7 and a compassionate E.

The universe vibrates.

The room rings silent.

Ching!

chapter 15

"Well, Jonathan, did you look inside the suitcase?"

"Yeah," I say to David O. H. Cosgrove II. "I looked."

"Any observations?"

"What about the rest of your life—all those other years?"

"They are packed away in other suitcases," David says. "These are the years I want to share with you."

"World War Two?"

"Yes, World War Two."

"What about it?"

"For a long time, Jonathan, I've needed to make peace with something. That's where you can help."

"Me?"

He nods. "Jonathan, something happened long ago . . ."

He looks blindly at me, about twelve degrees east of my face.

"Something bad?"

"It's not that simple."

"But you've had, like, sixty years to figure this out. What can I do in a few days?"

"Just listen. Take notes. Write."

"Write what?"

He shrugs. "Whatever you think is true."

"Hey, the truth is just the truth," I say. "It might not even be the truth."

"Jonathan, we'll get to all this in good time. Are you comfortable with old-fashioned paper and pens?"

"Yeah, I think I remember how to use a pen."

He points to a drawer. Inside are a box of Bics—not cheap plastic ballpoints but sleek metal-on-plastic retractables—and a stack of canary yellow legal pads wrapped in cellophane. He's ready for me, all right.

I peel open the packages, grab a pen and pad. Settle back in my chair.

"Well, then," David says, "anchors aweigh."

It's the blind leading the blind because I have no idea where this is going. I just start jotting and scrawling. Sometimes he gets winded—cancer winded—which is a mix of rattly lungs and haggardly tired.

At these times, I wait a minute or two until David recharges. About every half hour, he says, "I have to transact a little business with Mr. PEE-buddy." Then he reaches for the red bottle with the picture of the winking elf.

I duck into the corridor, trade smirks with Dreadlock sitting at the reception counter, step back in.

As I make notes about David's life, I add my own editorial comments:

Born Grosse Pointe, Michigan. (A fuck of a long time ago.)

Father: Electrical engineer. Not rich. Not poor. (Somewhere in the Wonder-bread middle.)

Mother: Second-grade teacher. Specialty: Hot cross buns with currants. (What are currants?)

Older sister: Anne. Plump. Glasses. Never laughed. Never married. Died of boredom in 1972.

Younger sister: Sarah. Skinny. Freckles. Laughs a lot. Lives in Coral Gables, Florida. Twenty-eight grandchildren. (Moral: Laughter and skinniness are the secrets to long life and fertility.)

Family dog: Gil. Wire-haired mutt. Hit by a laundry truck. "Saddest day of my childhood."

Boy Scouts. Paper routes. Baseball.

Winters: Skated on frozen ponds. Played ice hockey. Chipped a tooth.

Summers: Fished on Upper Peninsula. Cabin on Walloon Lake. Black flies. Learned to shoot. Birds. Squirrels. Quota of three bullets a day to teach accuracy.

Size twelve feet by age twelve.

Six foot three by age fourteen. Nicknames: Beanpole. Cornstalk. Later: Shafty.

Lettered in swimming. Broke high school records in freestyle and butterfly.

Graduated: Grosse Pointe High School. Report cards "peppered with gentleman's Cs and dubious Ds." But As in history and English.

First "official" girlfriend: Lillith Sparks of Grosse Pointe.

First "unofficial" girlfriend: Blue Feather Chang, an Iroquois Chinese living in a shack outside Petoskey, age uncertain. (Damn, I need an "unofficial girlfriend.")

Attended University of Michigan on swimming scholarship. Switched major from journalism to medicine back to journalism.

Heroes: Abraham Lincoln, Teddy Roosevelt, Lawrence of Arabia.

Favorite books: Great Expectations, The Jefferson Bible, The Boy Scout Handbook.

And so on.

All the way up to December 7, 1941.

I catch it all in my butterfly net. Everything. Not just the high points—the low points, the midpoints, and all the fractional points in between.

As a poet, I know that truth hides in the nuance.

Is the particle of gold in the bucket of sand.

You gotta sift.

Pan through a million grains to find it.

Right now, I haven't found much.

David Cosgrove's life is mostly sand. The start of it, anyway.

Just when it's getting good, when the Japanese pilots are slipping on their goggles and roaring off the flight decks of the *Kaga* and *Sōryū,* aiming for Pearl Harbor, David says, "That's enough for today, Jonathan."

He opens the drawer of his bedside table and pulls out an envelope.

"For you," he says.

I slip the envelope from his trembling hand.

"See you on Sunday, Jonathan."

"Adios, dude."

"Adios to you, too," he says. "Dude."

chapter 16

"Holy shit!"

The envelope contains three bank-crisp one-hundred-dollar bills. That's more than ten times what I expected.

Finally, somebody's paying me what I'm worth.

I soar past Dreadlock.

"How'd it go?"

"Phenomenal," I say, and keep on soaring.

Between buses, I duck into 7-Eleven and buy a twelve-pack of Red Bull. This time, I splurge and buy the tall 16-ounce cans, not the skinny little 8.3-ouncers. Also, I buy a big bottle of maximum strength NoDoz.

Trucker size. Guaranteed for long hauls.

I'm feeling pretty good: Ruby on my shoulder, Red Bull in my arms, a fortune in my pocket.

I'm standing in line behind three guys.

The guy up front is ordering a lottery ticket. Big and lunky, he grips a giant Target bag under his arm. Tufts of gray hair spill from under his ball cap. He's dressed in the greasy, baggy clothes of a tire mechanic.

Uh-oh.

I cock my head.

View him one degree at a time.

Ear—could be.

Jawbone—could be.

I lean farther out and see all the way to the chin. The bushy eyebrow.

Jeezus!

It's Vic.

I slip on my hood. Pull Ruby high onto my shoulder, hoping she'll cast a shadow.

Then I fade into the far aisle and ponder him over the SpaghettiOs and Wish-Bone dressings.

Biologically and technically, Vic is my father. But that raises the question: What is a father? A sperm-blasting shotgun? Or a shepherd who pulls the little lambs out of the quicksand and keeps the wolves away?

I vote for the shepherd. In which case, the guy buying the lottery ticket is definitely *not* my father.

I haven't seen him for nearly eight months—since the funeral. He sat two rows back, off to the side, alone, a brooding pastrami sandwich in a stained tie and shades.

Afterward, he walked up to me. Took off those shades.

"Why?" he asked.

Why!

"How?" would've been easy. Just quote the *Seattle Times:*

"A West Seattle teenager was struck and severely injured by a Metro bus late Tuesday . . . . 'He just shot out of the dark on his skateboard,' said veteran driver Griffin Delmorio. 'I didn't see him.'"

What the *Seattle Times* didn't say was this: that bus would've killed anyone else instantly. But Telly was too full of life to die instantly.

Or this: that Telly was on a mission to buy me a bottle of cold medicine.

When he offered to skate down, I said, "Yeah."

I could've said, "No."

But I said, "Yeah."

His whole life and future were tied to that one word, uttered by me.

A shrugged "Yeah."

Just as all our lives are tied to shrugged words and thin strings of mortality.

"Why?"

I turned and walked away from Vic.

Now he shifts the giant Target bag to his other arm, drops coins and wadded bills onto the counter. The clerk hands him the lottery ticket, slides two pecan snack pies and a motor magazine into a paper bag.

I zoom in on Vic's hands. Fat fingers.

I remember how he raised those hands. Made pretend swats. And real ones.

Tried to slow us down, shape us in his Cro-Magnon image. But he couldn't.

I look at my own hands. Are they getting a little chunky?

He heads for the door of 7-Eleven. I sink inside my hood.

As he passes, I glimpse inside the Target bag.

It's diapers. A forty-eight-pack of Huggies.

Uh-oh! The last thing a baby needs is Vic for a father.

chapter 17

When I get home, I pop a Bull. The taurine kicks right in.

Ah, taurine. I ponder the spelling: T-A-u-r-i-n-e.

It covers the basics: tits, ass, and piss.

I make a stockpile of all my projects. Spread 'em out before me, at least in my mind:

Homework: Cram for a Spanish III test. Read four chapters of *Talleyrand* and write a three-page essay, due next week. Read fifty-two pages of physics, quiz Thursday.

Murchison: Dig into the diaries and make copious notes (what I call "copu-noting"). Also, go through more photo albums. The good news is, this stuff is raw. Even though it's old and faded, it's fresh. As soon as you open an album or diary, you're right back there. Can feel the sun on your face and the wind off the waves.

"Tales of Telemachus": All I really want to do is work on this poem. If I could just shove all the other crap into a ditch, bury it with a bulldozer, and work on this poem, I'd be happy.

The girlfriend project: This skips along the garden path from mind to penis and back again. My mind likes one kind of girl, with poetic sensibilities, and my penis likes another, with poetic curves. Rarely do these two qualities merge in one girl. Result: confusion. I'm as virgin as Italian olive oil. There's a good reason happiness is not spelled "hap-penis."

The Pinky Toe project: It ain't crystallizing. "Crossing the

River Styx" is just as pussified as ever. And the thought of play-ing and singing in front of all those people scares the shit out of me. Basically, I can't do it. I won't do it. I'll tell Gupti—or write her a note.

Sleep: I'm going on day four without it. Thanks to taurine and caffeine, and heavy lacings of sucrose and glucose, I'm wired. But the wires are getting thinner. Think light bulb–filament thin.

To make it all happen, I've got to find a system—some new level of hyperefficiency. But what?

I'm pondering this when there's a knock on my door. Mimi comes in. She's wearing her tight-ass Levi's. She's barefoot and in the process of buttoning her blouse. I can see the fringes of her lacy bra and the cloven depths that drive the Thriftway dads wild. Today she's favoring green eye makeup.

"Listen, Jonathan, you've *got* to work on the house. We open in four and a half months."

Oh yeah, I can't forget "The Chapel of the Highest Happi-ness." I need to add that to my list. Mimi's romantic little dream. True, I haven't set foot on the scaffolding in two weeks. The south side of the house cries to be scraped. The entire house screams to be primed and painted.

"Later," I say.

"Later meaning in ten minutes?"

"Later meaning whenever."

"We can't wait that long, Jonathan. The season starts June first. Also, I want you to write me an ad for the *West Seattle Herald.* Just a little something about the chapel."

"Write your own damn ad!"

"You're the writer," she says.

"Hey, Mimi, look."

I fan my two remaining hundred-dollar bills and my four twenties.

Mimi gasps. If there's one god she worships, it's the god Cash. I don't mean Johnny.

"Did you turn Jesse James on me?"

"My new job," I say.

"That writing job?"

"Yeah."

She grins. "I told you, baby. White collar."

She leans in to take a closer look. Quick as a rattler, she strikes. Snaps away one of my Benjamins. Tucks it into her bra.

I start to lunge, but that's one place I'm not going.

"Ha!" she says victoriously. "If you want it back, you'll do three hours on the house, starting now."

How could I be so stupid!

I glance out the window. Perfect catch-pneumonia weather. It's getting dark. What kind of mom would send her kid out on a day like this? And I've got a ton of homework to do.

"You bi . . . witch."

"Yeah, you better say *witch*," Mimi says. "But a good witch—like Glinda in *The Wizard of Oz*. I promise to keep it cozy and warm."

"Hey, Mimi," I say, "does, uh, Vic have a girlfriend or maybe a new wife?"

Her face darkens. "How should I know?"

I shrug.

"Baby," she says, "get your butt scrapin'!"

chapter 18

To get my head in the right place for scraping, I pop a Bull and swallow three NoDoz. One thing about all this taurine and caffeine, I'm losing weight. Notching my belt tighter and tighter.

Last spring, before the accident, Telly and I stood and weighed about the same—five nine and one forty, give or take a pound or two.

I'm taller now, maybe five ten, but as for weight . . .

I go into the bathroom and step on the scale. The dial sways dreamily, then stops at one . . . twenty . . . seven. I tap the glass with my toe to see if the needle is stuck, but it seems to be working.

Down thirteen pounds. *Jeezus.*

I check in the mirror. My cheeks have hollowed. My face looks ashen. Or maybe that's just my hair casting a shadow.

To pack on some weight, I start thinking about apple pie for dinner. A whole one. And a half gallon of vanilla bean ice cream.

Mimi sure as hell isn't going to bake a casserole.

I lace into my painting shoes and slip on my spattered hoodie, loop an old wool muffler around my neck. Slip on my knuckle gloves. Spur of the moment, I speed dial Nick the Thick.

"Hey, dude, wanna make some money?"

"Be right over."

Fact is, Nick will work for the sheer pleasure and joy of hanging out with me. Why he likes me so much is a mystery. I don't like me half as much. But Nick, being younger by seven months, glommed on to Telly and me years ago, in the good ol' toddle days. Followed us around like a wagging puppy. Thought Telly was the glorious sun.

Smart as he is, a technological mind built on a platform of common sense, Nick's easy to exploit. Because he's so trusting. I hate to do that. I *will* pay him, eventually. (I think.)

I'm on the scaffolding, and it's drizzling. Correction: it's mizzling, which is a combination of mist and drizzle. Earlier, it was snizzling. These are important distinctions because, when you write, it's the little details that lift your wings. Birdwell likes to quote Mark Twain: "The difference between the right word and the almost right word is the difference between lightning and a lightning bug."

So it ain't a drizzle, it's a mizzle.

I'm scraping away, making pretty good time. Listening to Pinky Toe on my iPod. To my surprise, the tunes are pretty good. Born in a gut vortex, where all good tunes and poems are born.

All except "Crossing the River Styx." Gupti's favorite. It's born in a plastic clamshell. Fake as a silicone breast.

I could never handle the intro lick in front of a crowd. It's way too fast and frilly. It's gotta be pared down and bulked up. But how?

And how do I handle the vocal range? I'm a midrange singer, basically one octave, and this is at least a two-octave song that leaps into a ball-squeezing falsetto.

And how'm I gonna handle my nerves in front of all those people? Just the thought of the Kenny G—Taft's auditorium—stuffed with twelve hundred pie faces makes me shudder.

I dig into my pocket. Buried amid guitar picks and change is a hard wad of paper. I uncrumple the business card of Frank Conway, musician and music instructor.

Just then Nick shows up.

Kyle is with him. So is Jordan. So is Javon. They pile out of the VW bug.

They're wearing their soccer uniforms—white jerseys, red shorts. Only Nick—the best soccer player of them all—is dressed in his butt-lows and flannel shirt.

"Hell, what is this?" I say across the sodden grass. "Rodeo clown week?"

What I'm really thinking is *Great! My whole team. Now we can finish the south side of the house.*

They shamble up in half-laced shoes and floppy shin guards. I'm standing on the scaffolding like Jesus on the Mount. It's time to preach a sermon. I clear my throat:

"Our Father who art on Delridge Avenue, give us this day our daily bread. Only make it pumpernickel and slap on some French's mustard and cucumber chips."

They don't laugh. They don't smile.

"Holy Father," I say, "maybe you should make that focaccia."

"Shut up!" Kyle says.

Nobody's got even a glint of "smass," which is our special West Seattle blend of smart-ass and sass. They glare at me like moronic court bailiffs.

"Here, dudes," I say, offering my wrists, "I'm guilty."

In times of silence, when voids gape and leaders are born, no one speaks. That's because I'm the leader. Telly was, and by rightful ascension and hierarchy, I am now.

Except I'm not Telly. I'm no leader. I have the mouth, but I don't have the discipline or desire. And I'm no follower either. In between leader and follower is a vast empty prairie where nonleaders and nonfollowers wander alone among the tumbleweeds. Drooling nomads.

I am one of those.

Nick says, "Man, we're worried about you."

Nick can say no wrong, twist no truth. He is the shy, smiling compass that points true north, not fake magnetic north. Everybody respects him. Everybody nods.

Javon says, "Ever since—"

"Yeah, yeah," I say.

"It's like you're on drugs, man," Jordan says.

"I'm not on drugs. Unless you count taurine."

"Taurine?" they ask.

"A sulfonic acid," Nick says, "found in the stomachs of cows. What he means is, he's drinking a lot of Red Bull."

"Yeah," I say. "Very high performance. Enhances my cognitive skills. Plus it has all the essential food groups—caffeine, sugar, and bull sperm."

Nobody laughs.

Jordan says, "That why you're all scrawny and pale-lookin'? Why your voice shakes? Why you don't sleep at night—and can barely stay awake all day?"

"You do look scrawny, dude," Kyle says. "No offense."

"Gaunt," I say. "The correct word is *gaunt*."

Javon says, "You're gonna flunk, man, if you miss any more school."

"Hey, I haven't missed a class all week."

Jordan says, "We feel it, too. We have to deal with it, too. But it's been almost a year, man. Pull yourself together. Start living again."

"I *am* living. In my own way, I'm living."

I stare down at them. Now, instead of feeling like Jesus on the Mount, I feel like Jesus on the cross.

"Hey, I forgive you," I say. "You don't know what the hell you're talking about."

"Oh, we know what we're talking about," Kyle says.

Nick nods. "Yes, we do."

My earphones are dangling from my pocket. All through this trial, amid the drip-drop-plop of rain, I can hear Pinky Toe playing. The sound is puny and scratchy. The others begin to hear it, too. The song ends, and—wouldn't you know it—here comes Gupti's favorite.

Kyle points to my earphones. "What the hell's that?"

"A tune called 'Crossing the River Styx,'" I say.

"What?"

Nick laughs. "Perfect."

"Why's that so perfect?" Kyle asks.

"Styx—named after the river in Hades," Nick says. "Remember, in Miss Scardino's class, *The Odyssey:* when you cross the River Styx, you cross from life to death."

"Yeah," I say. "I'd like to jump into that river right now. Anybody wanna grab a towel and join me?"

"Not me," Javon says. "I don't wanna die."

"And what's all this I hear about graduation?" Kyle says. "You really gonna do some tune?"

"Yeah. As a matter of fact, this tune."

I toss him my iPod, and he plugs the little buds into his ears. At first, his face is thoughtfully bland, and then it darkens.

"This is a faggy old-man band," Kyle says.

"Yep," I say.

"He's doing it for Gupti," Nick says. "It's her favorite song."

"Then you better do it right," Jordan says, "if you wanna come back next year."

"Not sure what I wanna do next year," I say. "I might join the circus. Or climb Mount Everest."

"You gonna play the Ric?" Kyle asks.

Whoa! That's something I hadn't pondered. The Ric—the custom-built cherry red electric guitar that's smarter than me and all other humans. In my limited thinking on the subject, I'd seen myself playing Ruby, with a pickup or standing mike. But Ruby—my sweet little princess from Saskatchewan, pretty as she is, my own true love—is a shy wallflower compared to the Ric.

"I'm thinking about it," I say.

"Hold up!" Kyle says. He punches his palm. "Dudes, my mind is on fire."

We watch as flames engulf his mind.

"Listen," he says, "it's quite obvious that Jonathan needs our help and expertise, so we're gonna produce this little segment for him. I will personally be the director and executive in charge. Javon, you do the lights."

Javon nods. "Yeah, I can do that."

Both Kyle and Javon are taking Advanced Theater from

Miss Yan-Ling. And not just because her name means "voluptuous tinkling of jade pendants." Both of them have the gamer's touch with the control board—namely, speed and intuition. I've seen them work. Both are bold theatrical thinkers, especially Kyle, whose goal in life is to produce a Super Bowl halftime show starring Janet Jackson and some rapping chimpanzees.

The offer smacks of possibilities.

"We're talking the Kenny G—big stage, dudes," Kyle says. "Proscenium arch. *Whew!*"

Javon says, "Man, I could throw a pin on you and make you glitter like gold."

"Dudes!" Kyle says. "This is gonna be maximal."

"Hold up," I say. "I'm a minimalist."

Kyle nods. "One man's maximal is another man's minimal. But hey, I respect you as a fellow artist. However, you're gonna need help getting your stars in alignment." He smacks his palm again. "This is perfect."

"No, it ain't," I say.

My gut is sinking. Just the thought of facing all those people makes me sweat.

If Delridge Avenue were the River Styx, I'd dive in and swim across.

"The point is—" Kyle says.

"The point," Nick says, cutting him off, "is thickness forever."

Nick's words sink in.

We remember, silently. Standing in the fast-fading light on the scaffold or sodden grass, we remember Telly. If you cried for my brother, you are my thick. Go ahead and commit a felony against your grandmother, but you are my thick for life. You can't revoke that.

"Hey," I say. "Grab some scrapers and get to work."

"Can't," Kyle says, sweeping his hand across his soccer jersey. "Brotherhood of the team."

"Yeah," Jordan says, "we got a night game."

They tramp across the grass and fold themselves into the VW bug.

All but Nick, who stands there smiling after them.

"Don't you have soccer, too?"

Nick grabs a spar and swings onto the scaffolding. Suddenly, he's taller than me. Skinny as a skeleton, but wide shouldered. Perfect aerodynamic design for flight on a soccer field. He grabs the scraper from my hand.

"Only thing I like better than soccer," he says, "is scraping houses in the rain."

The rest of my team is gone.

But Nick the Thick . . .

Sticks.

chapter 19

Nick and I scrape like madmen. Darkness falls, and we're still scraping. Blindly. In the mizzly, moonless ink of West Seattle night, we are sponges of humanity, black, unrecognizable blobs. Hunchbacks of the scaffold. Brothers of the blade. Nothing stops us—not even four calls from Nick's increasingly pissed-off mom ordering him home for dinner.

Each time she calls, something aches inside me. Nick has a warm home and kitchen to go back to. He has homemade lasagna waiting for him, probably slathered with extra cheese. He has a mom who knows what moms do. A dad who knows what dads do.

He has a little brother and sister. All his people are in place.

The way he shrugs it off seems careless, almost cruel.

If I had a home like that to go to, I'd pitch my scraper at the sky and retire from my drooling nomadism.

I'd be so damn happy.

But all I have is Mimi.

We finish the south side of the house, and Nick slips away before I can buy that apple pie. This depresses me, and I lose my appetite.

I go up to my room, peel off my wet clothes, put on a dry T-shirt and boxers, and get under my quilt. Everything starts calling to me. My books. Murchison. My poems. It's like they have their own puny voices, and my room has become a Tower of Babel.

I pop a Bull and reach for my Spanish text. As I settle back I hit the remote. *Rush Hour 3* is just starting. Jackie Chan and Chris Tucker have landed in Paris. I decide to multitask.

For the next two hours, I'm amazingly efficient. My thirst for taurine is opening my mind to new realities. What I discover is this: All knowledge is built upon transitions. Whether it's Spanish or the French Revolution or physics, the focus is on change.

So as I study, I rev my brain each time a chapter pivots— whether it's discussing the conjugation of Spanish verbs, main currents in eighteenth-century French political thought, or wave patterns.

I call my discovery "Transition Theory."

Following the principles of Transition Theory, I blast through Spanish, physics, and Talleyrand, skipping huge chunks of text that seem merely trivial or repetitious.

My theory applies to *Rush Hour 3,* too. All of the key scenes are sharp-focused action, and everything else is just patter or buildup. I realize that if you edit the movie according to Transition Theory, you have about eighteen minutes of pivotal moments in both dialogue and action. All you really need are those eighteen minutes—that pure essence. Forget the other seventy-five minutes—the jokes, the scenes in the taxi, the sex. They are unnecessary.

Well, maybe the sex is necessary.

Transition Theory may be the key to my survival.

Yippee-aye-oh-cuy-ay.

A little after midnight, I toss my books aside and pull Murchison over to my bed.

I dig out a thick gray folder labeled "Sinking of the USS *Gabriel Trask.*" The folder is full of official files and documents. And more photos. As usual, the photos are black-and-white snapshots of sailors. By now, I recognize some of them:

The tall sailor with dark, curly hair.

The stocky sailor with light hair.

The sailor who looks like Arnold Schwarzenegger from the bellybutton up and Mickey Mouse from the bellybutton down.

A wind snaps through nearly every photo. You can see it in their hair and uniforms. Other photos show them in port cities, with the names inked below: Wellington, Sydney, Nouméa.

Nouméa? Where the hell is that? I Google it—capital city of New Caledonia, a French territory in the South Pacific.

Sailors with their arms around girls, grinning at the camera.

Sailors, sailors, everywhere.

Drink enough taurine and those grainy black-and-whites come to life, like one of the old newsreels Mr. Mandelheim shows in history class.

I start to think of these guys as thicks. Like my own thicks. Curly, Shorty, and Arnold aren't too different from Kyle, Nick, and Javon.

If my thicks and I could swim back in time, right onto the deck of the USS *Gabriel Trask,* we'd fit right in. Time and fashion may change; thickness does not. Thickness is one of the few constants in the universe.

What makes you thick? It's a mix of things—sharing major

experiences, sharing day-to-day stuff, through many seasons, and relating to them, and each other, with instinctive honesty. Getting mad at each other and forgiving.

Plus that edge that is sometimes sharp, sometimes rubbery, depending on your mood.

And, of course, getting used to each other's farts.

Thickness is everywhere, among young and old, on street corners and on school playgrounds. I'm very conscious of it. I even see it as a color—soft blue.

The dudes at the Alamo were thick.

Odysseus and his men were thick.

The sailors in the pictures are probably dead, or ninety, but their thickness lives on.

Thickness transcends death. Is an eternal torch.

If you are not thick with someone, you are very much alone in the world.

Still, even thickness can't always shed light on a truly dark soul.

And mine is truly dark.

Deeper in the files is a document entitled "War Department Inquest." The subtitle is "Examination into the deaths of thirteen sailors aboard the USS *Gabriel Trask*, 7 April 1945. Based on the testimony of Lt. David O. H. Cosgrove, USN."

The document is 152 pages long.

The last page, entitled Glossary D, is a list of the thirteen sailors by name, age, rank, serial number, address, and next of kin. They pretty much represent a cross section of the country: Bozeman, Montana; Truro, Massachusetts; Wink, Texas; Los Angeles, California.

And so on.

I peel off another Bull. Pop a Doz. Gargle it down. Pull the light closer. Settle back on my pillow.

Then I load some Transition Theory into my brain. Let the rest of the world sleep—I'm swimming back to April 1945.

chapter 20

Out David's window, it's raining. The afternoon is dark and drippy. A bit Dickensian. A bit Stygian. Very Seattle-ian. The birch trees across the street wave their tendrilly fingers at me. Every few seconds, the third tree on the left rotates its wrist and flips the bird at me.

"Fuck you, Jonathan! . . . Suck it, Jonathan! . . . Go jump off a bridge, Jonathan!"

Since we started our little project, I've watched those hands sprout green mittens.

I've watched David's shoulders drop more and more—sloped by the totality of his illnesses and years.

I've listened to his mucous cough hack away at his ribs till they seem ready to break.

The Delphi is hell's putrid gutter. But deeper inside are doorways to other places, like Agnes's world or the South Pacific.

And these places I can handle. In fact, I would almost rather be there than anyplace else.

Today, David sits in his wheelchair. Buttoned in his tattered old-man sweater. Trying to get his breath back. He stares blindly at the floor.

Pretty soon, he lifts his cup. Sucks shaved ice through a straw to "lubricate" his vocal chords. Then he starts to talk again. Many words arrive cracked or scratched.

I start copu-noting on the canary yellow legal pad.

Jot this idea for a bumper sticker: "I'd rather be copu-lating."

On average, I fill one legal pad with my copu-noting per session. So far, I've filled thirty-one legal pads. Stuffed them into my backpack or Ruby's zippered pocket. But I haven't written a single word of David's book. *Not a single word!*

Maybe I could just type up my notes. Garnish them with some poetic parsley. I could power myself with twelve-packs of taurine and write that damn book in one marathon session, sprinting the whole twenty-six miles.

But Gupti would see through it.

Birdwell would see through it.

I would see through it.

"Finishing is what you have to do," Ernest Hemingway said. "If you don't finish, nothing is worth a damn."

Unfortunately, that's probably true.

Telly said, "Don't do anything half-assed. Do it full-assed. Ten on a scale of ten. Angelina Jolie."

Both Ernest and Telly are right.

But exactly what does "finishing" and "full-assed" mean?

David Cosgrove's life is an endless series of details and facts, with something missing. A crossword puzzle where the border pieces are linked, but the inside is a gaping hole.

A cave where he's hiding something. He's been hiding it from me for four months. Now he wants to bring it out in the open, the sunlight, and he doesn't know how. He's just too damn stuck to the back of that cave.

But hey, I know a little about caves myself.

I can't talk full-assed about Telly, because words just don't do the job. The soul is a canyon, and the English language is a rope that goes down only so far, then leaves you dangling.

Maybe if I could sleep, not just catnap or skim the surface. Yeah, sleep.

The only place I *can* sleep—sink into REM, if only for forty-five minutes—is in the furnace room at Taft, in that narrow slot, about the size of a coffin, between the brick wall and the furnace. Knowing José is nearby. Keeping a safe eye. Keeping that old stove humming and thrumming.

José—Janitor God of Sleep, Lord Protector of Comatose Teenagers.

A man in coveralls doing the work of Zeus. Scraping by on a poverty salary. He should be the highest-paid employee in the school district.

Right now, I don't feel sleepy because I've just transfused twelve ounces of taurine into my blood. But I know my body craves sleep—Marianas Trench deep sleep. Where owl-eyed fish glide silent and spineless. Deeper than light.

chapter 21

When I walk into the Delphi about 1:45 p.m. on Sunday, Dreadlock's chair is empty. This throws me because she's always there, and I figure she's just stepped away. Maybe to tweak her "dreads."

So I sit in the lounge among the soon-to-die and listen to the laughing TV. Is there a hollower sound in the world? Can death be worse than this?

I wait for her. Wait twenty minutes, but no Dreadlock.

No Dreadlock means no Agnes. No Agnes means no Ruby the Lute.

Ruby rests sadly on my shoulder. Zipped in her gig bag.

A beautiful guitar, like a beautiful girl, needs to be unzipped and plucked.

That is my motto. In Latin:

Guitarus unzippus pluckus.

I'm getting used to playing for Agnes. When everything is right and in tune and my voice is on key, she falls into her chanting. It doesn't matter what I play—the theme from "SpongeBob SquarePants" or something from *American Idiot*— Agnes gets into it. She starts her mantra. Claps in time. Chants:

Free the swimmers in the dark.
Free the swimmers in the dark.

We could do a whole CD of Agnes chanting, with me throwing in guitar licks all the way from folk to funk.

Guaranteed not to sell.

What I like about playing for Agnes is, she doesn't see *me* when I play. She just hears the music. So after a minute, I can get into it. Forget about everything else. Forget about my ego, whether I'm any good or not. Just play.

Flat Ass waddles over and sits in Dreadlock's chair. She's all potato and no gravy. When the flat asses of the world take over from the tight ones, some god somewhere must be weeping.

So I leave the laughing TV, leave the thought of Dreadlock and Agnes, of guitars and lutes, and go to David Cosgrove's room. Lean sad Ruby in a corner. Pull out a fresh canary yellow legal pad and a Bic retractable.

And begin my scrawling day.

• • •

In David's mind, there is only one war: "The War"— World War II.

Not Iraq. Not Afghanistan. Not Vietnam. Not Korea.

One war.

David talks about life on a "tin can." Specifically, about life on his tin can, DD-414, the destroyer USS *Gabriel Trask*.

"It's not like a movie, Jonathan, starring John Wayne or what's-his-name, George Clooney. For every day of action, there were hundreds of days of boredom, where we did nothing but wait. Or drill. For the most part, Jonathan, drill and drudgery are the linchpins of the sailor's life. But then, in the last months of the war . . . my god, my god . . ."

"Tell me about April sixth, 1945."

David's head jerks. His blind eyes home in on me.

"It's almost time, Jonathan."

"Hey," I say, "it's way past time."

"If there's one day that defines me, Jonathan, it's April sixth, 1945, and the morning of April seventh. Have you ever had a day that defines you? An end-of-the-world-as-you-know-it day? A kind of Armageddon?"

"Yeah, thirteen months ago."

"Your brother?"

"Yeah."

"What was the date?"

"April seventeenth—that's the day he got hit. He died twenty-five days later on May twelfth. All those days were Armageddon."

"I'm sorry, Jonathan."

"What about April sixth, 1945?"

"All the facts are in the inquest report."

"Yeah, I know the facts," I say. "Your ship got blasted and some guys died. But there's a lot I don't know."

"That's true, Jonathan. The inquest report, the newspaper accounts—they don't begin to tell the full story."

"Words never do," I say. "They're supposed to, but they suck."

David nods. "Yes, words can get in the way. We shoot at the duck, but we often miss."

"Shoot at the duck?"

"Seek the true meaning, Jonathan."

"*Whew!*" I say. "I've never hit that duck either. Not even once. People say I have, in my poems, but I haven't."

"Maybe we don't need to hit the duck, Jonathan. Maybe all we need to do is say what we must say once, to another human being, openly and honestly, with humility and remorse. Maybe that is enough."

I ponder this. "Yeah, maybe."

"Jonathan, I want you to go back to the inquest report and focus on pages one hundred to one forty."

"You mean the battle?"

"I mean the *aftermath* of the battle."

Aftermath.

It's not a place I want to go. I skipped that section of the report—Transition Theoried myself right on to the next section. But David seems ready to go there, and I know we have to. He's talked around the edges long enough. He's ready to shoot at the duck.

Well, almost.

"Next time," he says, "we will talk about the aftermath."

"Yeah," I say. "Let's take a few potshots at that duck."

"Yes," David says.

"Promise?"

"Promise."

"But today," he says, "we will talk about 'Iceberg.'"

So today we go back to April 1, 1945.

The *Gabe* is steaming toward Okinawa, part of a giant task force—part of something called "Operation Iceberg."

"We arrived off Hagushi Beach," David remembers. "Everything felt different this time. The stakes higher. We desperately needed Okinawa. It was to be our steppingstone to the home islands of Japan—to ultimate invasion. The enemy knew this and was equally desperate to repulse us. On April first, we patrolled north of Ishima. On April third, fourth, and fifth, we escorted a convoy headed to Ulithi."

On and on David talks. Till his voice—like a dimming flashlight—runs down to nothing.

Finally, he rasps, "Enough."

I shove the legal pad into my backpack. Stand and shoulder Ruby. David reaches into his table drawer, pulls out an envelope.

"Jonathan . . ."

His hand trembles.

I grab the envelope. Peek inside.

Shake my head. "Dude, this is way too much."

"Goodbye, Jonathan."

"Well, thanks."

"Oh, Jonathan?"

"Yeah?"

"Katie's taken a turn for the worse."

"You mean the receptionist?"

He taps his vocal chords. Recharges them a bit. "Katie's not our receptionist. She lives here."

"Lives here?"

"Yes, she's part of our community. Didn't you know?"

"No—yeah! I mean, she's no ordinary receptionist. What's she got?"

"She has the Mother Teresa gene," David says.

"Is that some kind of cancer?"

"It's her way of looking at life, Jonathan. It'll see her through everything, including this latest reaction to chemo." He smiles. "She's down the hall in one forty-seven. Say hello on your way out. Give her my fond regards."

chapter 22

The door to room 147 is open. A nurse stands inside, checking monitors, jotting notes.

Katie lies in bed, hooked to tubes.

Skinned-potato bald. Big bruise on her IV arm.

Her wigs rest on mannequin heads in a small bay window. One is black ropes of dreadlocked hair. One is bowl-cut Day-Glo-blue hair. One is long Beyoncé-brown hair.

The nurse looks up from her clipboard.

"Who are you?"

"Good question," I say.

"It's okay," Katie says.

I shamble in, Ruby on one shoulder, backpack on the other. I'm too frayed and disheveled to be standing in such a clipboard-efficient room, one so tidy and well lit.

The nurse leaves, flashing five fingers. "You have *five minutes.*"

Katie sneers at her back, mouth-echoes *five minutes.*

Like David, she's got a transparent oxygen tube connecting her nose to a little green tank on the floor.

"Stare all you want."

"No thanks."

I step to the window.

The view is of Schmitz Park—deep ravine, big trees, trails. A spoonful of Telly lives in Schmitz Park, where Grandpa took us to see the last of the old growths, pick the blackberries of August.

Grandpa—he lived his last eighteen months in a senior care facility. Called it "an old folks' home," which made the other old folks grind their teeth. He was a dedicated smoker, a coughing shifter of gunk from one charred lung to the other. Wore his white hair long, hippie-poet-style, like Walt Whitman.

"Only three things in this world I cherish," he used to say. "Jasper and you boys."

Jasper was his Border collie, a fat, limping wreck of a dog.

Grandpa spent a good part of every morning standing on a strip of grass on Delridge Avenue waiting for Jasper to poop. And waiting . . . and waiting.

Love is patient, I guess.

Or constipated.

He was not one to scoop. "Dogs been crappin' on grass since Neanderthal times. You think those knuckle draggers scooped shit? Why mess with tradition?"

Grandpa wasn't too popular with the local residents.

I think he cherished Mimi, too, but it's not easy when you're both cut from the same spool of barbed wire.

"I know this for sure," Grandpa told us. "You boys will stride across far bigger ground than I ever did."

I'm grateful to god, the seven fates, and the thirteen furies that Grandpa never lived to know about Telly.

It would've killed him.

"Which of my heads do you like best?" Katie asks.

I gaze at the three faceless mannequin heads. Touch the long Beyoncé hair, rub a strand between my fingers.

"This one."

"Typical."

"How's it typical?"

"Never mind. Play me something."

"No way. That nurse'll kill me."

"We all gotta die sometime, Jonathan."

"Yeah," I say. "We do."

I slide Ruby out of her gig bag. No good chairs in the room, so I move the mannequin heads and perch my scrawny ass on the sill of the bay window. Fish a pick from among my pennies.

My repertoire isn't big enough to take requests, but I do like to match the music with the moment. Best way is to start noodling and let your instincts decide. So I play a C chord and stumble onto an old trail, something I haven't played in forever, right out of the beginner's song book: "Oh! Susanna."

I pick it rusty and messy. Then I pick it again, to clean it up. Third time, I hammer a couple of notes, bend a string. Give Stephen Foster a squeeze of blues juice.

Thing about bending strings, you bend every one, it sounds like crap. You bend one or two, it sounds good.

More is less, less is more.

True of poetry, too.

Maybe of life itself. I haven't worked that one out yet.

While I'm messing around with Ruby, Katie's eyes glaze over. She doesn't seem to mind the tune. Fact, I can see she likes it. Because she's smiling about two percent.

I pick it, hammer it, chord it, bend it.

When I stitch it up, she says, "Jonathan, everybody at the Delphi has good days and bad. Just like you."

"Yeah," I say. "But most of my days are bad."

"Most of my days are good," Katie says. "Play it again."

This time, I slow it down.

When you play "Oh! Susanna" slowly and bend a string or two, it feels like ancient America—swamps and snakes and buggies and dirt roads and moonlit kisses. It's Walt Whitman whistling down the magnolia path. It's Abe Lincoln swinging his ax in the Illinois woods. It's Kurt Cobain playing the opening licks to "All Apologies." You hear a thousand ghostly voices in that melody.

You can play it folk, rock, grunge, hip-hop, blues, any way.

But slow is best.

It's not like I knew this ten minutes ago. But I know it now.

All the time I'm playing, I'm keeping a nerve tuned for the nurse.

Pretty soon, I don't care anymore. Let her come.

Let her hear "Oh! Susanna."

She could use a dose of the shaggy old blues, played West Seattle–style, on a guitar from Saskatchewan that thinks she's a lute.

In fact, "Oh! Susanna" might be part of the cure. Just what the Delphi needs. Music that transcends time, place, and disease.

Katie never lets go of that two-percent smile.

Even when she dozes off, her breathing tube wrapped over her ear.

chapter 23

"Dude," Kyle says. "Let me do all the talking."

We're standing in the Kenny G waiting for Miss Yan-Ling. The Kenny G is Taft's performing arts center. It's named after Kenneth Gorelick, a Seattle-born saxophone player who holds the world record for playing the longest note ever recorded on a saxophone, an E-flat, which he held for forty-five minutes and forty-seven seconds in 1997 at J&R Music World in New York City.

The Kenny G is more than twice as big as the Quincy Jones over at Garfield High School. It can seat a thousand people. But you can add a couple hundred folding chairs without blocking the fire exits.

The Kenny G was designed by egos for egos.

I'm not an ego. If I have to play, give me a no-tech theater that seats twelve people, all deaf grandmothers.

I follow Kyle upstairs onto the stage. It's still a few weeks to showtime, but damn, I'm already shaking. My body, my voice, my whole being.

Javon's up in the control booth, messing with the lights. He throws a pin on me. Suddenly, all of me is blue, even my orange T-shirt. Then I'm all green. Then all red.

"Hey, man," I shout into the glare, "enough with the rainbow."

"Listen up, dude," Kyle says. "I wanna put you above the stage. For maximum impact."

"Above the stage?"

"Relax," Kyle says. "Javon backs me up one thousand percent. DON'T YOU, JAVON?"

From up in the booth, behind the blinding glare, Javon's voice comes down, puny but clear.

"One thousand percent, dude."

Kyle throws his arms up and shouts, "Raise the backdrops."

Motors and pulleys start grinding. Slowly, one by one, the stage backdrops rise: the painted fire escape from *West Side Story,* the painted cornfield from *Oklahoma!,* the painted jukebox and soda fountain from *Grease.* Finally we see into the deep recesses of the stage, all the way past the ropes and Roman shields and mops and buckets and fake horses.

Standing against the back wall, tall as the highest furled curtain, is a statue of King Kong. Kyle is pointing directly at it.

"Do you see what I see?"

"The Velcro Kong?"

He nods. "The Velcro Kong, dude."

Kong glares at us with painted-orange eyes. All these years in the dusty back shadows, and he's still got it: primeval mystery; the potential to chew you up and spit you out, limb by limb.

Fact is, the giant prop is all that remains of a musical production of *King Kong,* which Taft presented back in 1999, a millennium ago. Kong is covered in black Velcro to catch the sponge-tipped spears.

"See that left paw, man," Kyle says.

"It's a hand, dude."

"Whatever, dude. I'm gonna put you and the Ric up there."

Kong has one arm dragging to his knee. The other he holds chest high, with the hand flat, palm up. It's supposed to be for holding the girl, but the position makes him look more like a TV pitchman for Dove soap.

"You want me to stand up there and play the Ric?"

"Yeah, and sing, too," Kyle says.

"Dude," I say, "you are one hundred percent delusional."

Kyle grabs my shoulder. Massages it. Slowly and profoundly, eyeball to eyeball, he says, "There is a fine line, dude, between delusion and genius."

"Hello, boys."

Here comes Miss Yan-Ling down the aisle. She's young and foxy. Of the seven hundred sixty-two thousand words in the English language, the one that best describes her is *pert*. Here's how I define *pert:* the state of being properly dressed while your body aches to be undressed.

Miss Yan-Ling climbs onto the stage. Peers up toward the control booth, shields her eyes against the glare. Lifts her voice theatrically. "Hello, Javon."

Way up in his techno-nest, Javon flickers *Hello.*

She turns to us, glances at her watch. "I've got seven minutes until Senior Improv. Go."

Kyle shifts on his feet. "Uhh . . . umm . . ."

She holds up her hand. "Kyle, let's take it from the top. And this time, expunge all prehistoric grunts from your vocabulary."

Kyle nods. "Yeah, well, see, Dr. Jacobson wants Jonathan to do this little tune at graduation."

"Yes, I know all about it," Miss Yan-Ling says, glancing at

me. "You're performing 'Crossing the River Styx' by Pinky Toe. A wonderful choice. What do you need from me?"

"Well, see, I've got some ideas for staging—like, you know, some of that philosophical theater stuff you've been teaching us."

"Can you please be more specific?"

Kyle rubs his chin. "Like that Stanislavsky dude says, live the part. Reach inside your caveman self. I mean, we wanna make it real and spontaneous. Who wants to see Jonathan just standing there with a guitar?"

Miss Yan-Ling smiles. "It's wonderful that you're taking initiative, Kyle. Konstantin Stanislavsky was one of the theater's greatest creative thinkers. Ideas are nothing if they do not achieve fruition through action. Are you all on the same page with this?"

Kyle nods. "Me and Javon agree one thousand percent."

"The question is, does Jonathan agree one thousand percent?"

All eyes shift to me. Miss Yan-Ling's are friendly and pert, Kyle's are parallel lasers. I can even feel Kong glaring at me from the back shadows. Up in the control booth, Javon has stopped messing with the lights. Steady purple.

Damn! In the deck of life, thickness is the highest trump card.

"One thousand percent," I say.

Kyle turns the lasers off.

Miss Yan-Ling smiles maternally, even though she's only about eight years older than us.

"Wonderful!" she says. "Kyle, you are now the producer of Jonathan's segment of the graduation ceremony. Do I need to see storyboards?"

"Nah," Kyle says. "It's simple."

"Well, keep me posted on all major decisions. Is that all?"

"Um," Kyle says. "Jonathan wants to play the Ric."

"The Ric? Oh, you mean the Rickenbacker guitar. But that's not really possible . . . it's more of a . . . you know, it's quite valuable . . . a museum piece, actually . . . hmmm . . . if anything were to happen . . . the liability . . . I don't see how . . . but then again . . . ." She sighs. "Let me think about it."

Because of the Kenny G's incredible acoustics, Javon overhears every last stuttered syllable. Each time Miss Yan-Ling changes thoughts, he changes lights. In the course of fifteen seconds, he flashes the whole spectrum at her, but she's too full of pondering to notice.

"With all due respect," Kyle says, "if anybody's gonna play the Ric, it oughta be Jonathan."

Miss Yan-Ling eyes me sadly. "Yes, it ought to." She reaches out and squeezes my shoulder. "Jonathan, how are you?"

"Phenomenal."

She sighs. "I loved how Telly used to stroll down the hall strumming his guitar. But I've never heard you play."

I'm about to say, "I fully suck," when Kyle breaks in.

"Trust me, Carlos Santana would take notes."

"Wonderful," Miss Yan-Ling says. "I can hardly wait to hear you perform." Then she exhales dramatically. "Oh, go ahead. Play the Ric. Just don't damage it."

"Guaranteed," Kyle says.

She glances at her watch. "Oh my god!"

"Wait," Kyle says. "We're gonna need a prop from one of the old musicals."

Miss Yan-Ling's already halfway down the stage stairs. She

waves an arm, meaning, I think, "Go ahead." But it might mean "No time to discuss."

"Thanks!" Kyle shouts as she races up the aisle and out the door.

A grin spreads across his face. Up in the control room, Javon rolls some knobs and the whole stage begins to spin in a Ferris wheel of prismatic light.

"Show's on," Kyle says, grabbing my arm and bumping my fist. "You, me, all us thicks—and the Velcro Kong—we're gonna make history here at Taft High School."

He beats his chest gorilla-style.

I'm thinking:

Dear Lord, please get me out of my life.
Buy me a ticket to the nearest monastery.
All I want to do is till the broccoli fields.

chapter 24

"Today," David says, "we will travel to some dark places. We will talk about death. And life."

"Wait, man," I say, "*you* will talk about death and life. I'm gonna sit here and take notes."

David says, "I'd rather this be a dialogue, Jonathan."

I shrug. "Okay by me."

"Did you read those pages of the inquest report?"

"Yeah."

Which is true. No Transition Theory this time. Just old-fashioned reading.

"Tell me, Jonathan, what was the state of the Pacific War in April 1945?"

"Well, uh, everything was kind of desperate, building to the grand finale, like in a movie."

"True," David says. "We were a few months away from dropping the A-bombs on Hiroshima and Nagasaki and the surrender aboard the *Missouri*. But those few months were like facing a wounded tiger that rises one last time to kill, and kill in a frenzy."

"You mean those last battles?"

"That's right," David says. "Those last battles—Iwo Jima and Okinawa—were among the most fierce naval engagements of the war. My ship, the *Gabriel Trask*, served on radar picket duty—the front lines—during both. On April sixth, 1945, off

Okinawa, the Japanese launched an air attack against the U.S. fleet. We were hit by a suicide plane."

"You mean a kamikaze?"

"Yes, a kamikaze."

"Jeezus."

"I remember that day, Jonathan, more clearly than yesterday."

"Hey," I say, "that's a bloodcurdling cliché."

"Call it what you will," David says, "but it's true. I can run the whole day through my mind like film through a movie projector. I see it all. Vividly."

"What do you see?"

"Well, for example, during breakfast that morning, our cook, Isaac Jackson, spilled boiling grease on his hand. He went off to sickbay and came back wearing a bear-paw-size bandage. We all laughed, because now all he was qualified to do was stir the mush. And I remember the sunrise—an explosion of red and orange. You know the old seaman's saying:

Red sky at morning,
sailor take warning.

"And standing on the bridge gazing at Okinawa Island through binoculars. Seeing how ultra blue the water was, how lush green the hills. And thinking, here I was, looking at paradise—and calculating whether our shells could reach its shore. Just before eight o'clock—"

"You mean oh eight hundred hours?"

"Yes, Jonathan, that's how we said it. Just before oh eight hundred hours, the Klaxon sounded."

"Klaxon?"

"The ship's siren, sounding general quarters."

"Oh, yeah."

"We scrambled to our battle stations. To the northeast, at about ten o'clock—meaning angle of altitude—we saw a hornet's nest of attack planes. I had command of the forty-millimeter guns. As the planes began to dive, going mainly for the big prizes—the carriers *Enterprise* and *Bunker Hill*—we opened up. One plane split off, climbed nearly straight up, and dove at us."

"Whoa!" I say. "What's that feel like?"

"It's a hypnotic thing, Jonathan. For a moment, I just stared. The idea of self-annihilation is totally foreign to the Western mind."

"Not totally," I say. "Suicide happens here, too."

"Yes, it does, Jonathan. But in our culture, taking your life is more an act of Yankee individualism. To be ordered to annihilate yourself for an abstraction like duty or country, without a fighting chance, that is alien to us. Think how different that pilot was from me and my crewmates. He was locked inside his cockpit. No parachute. No landing gear. Death was his destiny that day, and he knew it. We, on the other hand, were fighting for our survival. Our motive was much stronger."

"Maybe it's not that simple," I say. "Maybe he didn't really want to die."

"He probably didn't, Jonathan."

"So you shot him down?"

David nods. "While we were blasting away, a second plane was sneaking around to the east, hoping to hide in the sun. It banked—a rather beautiful chandelle—and came straight at us, low, no more than ten or fifteen feet off the water. We could see the torpedo strapped to its belly. See the dot that was the pilot. Zooming in on us."

"Hey," I say, "killing is something I could never do."

"Oh yes, you could," David says. "That dot may have been a human being, but one with a mind bent on our destruction. We gave him all we had. Poured lead into him—there's a blood-curdling cliché for you. But we couldn't bring him down."

David is back there, aboard his ship. He holds his fists together. They shake in staccato:

"Blekkity-blekkity-blek."

"Ka-blam!" I say.

David lowers his hands. "He slammed straight into us. The explosion knocked me to the deck. When I looked up, the sky was filled with churning black smoke. Everything smelled of fuel oil and exploded gunpowder. Fire crews were rushing about. We were in full damage control."

"But nobody got killed, right?"

"Oh, there was plenty of carnage, Jonathan. We sustained about forty dead and wounded. You're thinking of the men directly under my command. No, none of them was badly hurt. We'd been insulated by the heavy-plated armor in the gun nests. In that sense, we were lucky, for the time being."

"Did you start sinking?"

"The possibility of sinking was very real," David says. "I could see the captain on the bridge, through the smoke. He shouted: 'Lieutenant Cosgrove, is your crew intact?' I gave him a thumbs up. He shouted: 'Do whatever it takes to keep us afloat.' So I took my gunners down the ladders, through the smoke, to where the hull was damaged."

"How do you stop a ship from sinking?"

"You begin by sealing off the damaged compartments. Then you get the submersible pumps going."

"Shouldn't you have stayed up on deck and shot down some more kamikazes?"

"We had other gun crews, Jonathan. The captain weighed his options and made the call. We were needed below."

"Were those guys your friends?"

David starts to speak. Stops. It's not an easy question for him.

"An officer does not befriend the rank and file, Jonathan. But even today I could tell you every man's first, middle, and last name, where he was born, where he lived, who his girl-friend was. I'd served with them night and day for more than three years. But I didn't think of them as my friends."

"But all those pictures—didn't you take them?"

"Yes, I was quite a shutterbug in those days."

"Seems like they were your friends."

"They were more like my family, Jonathan. As their commanding officer, I was responsible for them."

"Are they the same guys listed at the back of the inquest report?"

"Yes."

"So what happened?"

"We ran the hoses topside. Started the pumps. Filled the damaged compartments with empty ammo cans, for flotation. The captain's plan was to crawl to a nearby island base called Kerama Retto, get patched up, then limp to Pearl Harbor for repairs."

"Long way to limp."

"Yes, but we were too busy trying to survive minute by minute to think about that. Remember, we were fighting two battles.

One above the water line—wave after wave of kamikazes—and one below, against the sea."

"Could you hear all that stuff going on outside, like the planes buzzing you and all that?"

"All too well."

"Were you scared?"

"Yes, Jonathan. I remember standing up to my waist in seawater, thinking, *Here's where I'll die. This is my tomb.*"

"What did you do?"

"I put my fears aside. Buried them."

"You can do that—bury your fears?"

"You have to, Jonathan."

"What was it like down there, in the bottom of the ship?"

"Well, imagine going down an old mineshaft, hearing it creak and strain, knowing it might cave in at any moment. But we had a job to do. You can't think about yourself; you've got to think about the entire crew."

"Was it dark?"

"No, we had lights. Our generators still functioned."

"What about all the dead guys? Did you dump them in the ocean?"

"You mean, did we commit them to the sea? No. A tender came alongside. They were moved to a transport vessel, to be returned to the States for proper burial."

"What about the wounded guys?"

"They were moved to a hospital ship, the USS *Relief.*"

"But you guys survived? I mean, your ship did."

"Yes, Jonathan. The *Gabe* was a casualty, not a fatality, of the suicide raid at Okinawa on April sixth."

"What about . . . ?"

David holds up his hand. "Enough for today, Jonathan."

"Yeah," I say. "Me too. My hand's about to break off."

"Let's save our strength for next time. We have deeper places to go. Darker places to swim."

"Adios," I say.

"Adios, Jonathan."

chapter 25

On my way down the corridor, I poke my head into room 114.

"Hey, Agnes."

She's sitting in her wheelchair, bundled in a bathrobe. The TV flashes colored shadows onto her face. On the screen, a model-perfect brunette is screaming tearfully at a model-perfect man. They fall into each other's arms and kiss.

Agnes grins at me. "Float a turd."

Of all the greetings in the world, this is now my favorite. "Float a turd" flings open a door and shouts that life is full of irony and madness. Is both beautiful and stinky.

We should all say it, from the president and Cabinet on down. Make it our national greeting.

Float a turd, everybody!

"Hey, Agnes, what do you mean, 'swimmers in the dark'?"

Her eyes brighten.

"You must free them."

"Free who?"

She points at me. "You know."

"No, actually, I don't."

"It's why you're here. To free the swimmers in the dark."

"Agnes," I say, "I've got a confession: I don't always get you."

She grins. "I'm ninety-nine years old. I want to be an angel."

"Hey," I say, "maybe you can do your oracle thing for me sometime. You know, let me know how it all turns out."

She meets my eye. "Never give up."

"Maybe sometimes," I say, "you have to."

"No, never," she says. "Never, ever, ever."

"But . . ."

The TV draws her back. The soap opera couple is still kissing. They're talking-kissing, kissing-talking. Cheeks polished with tears. Eyes lit with smiles.

Someday, I want to write for the soaps. It seems pretty easy.

"Adios, Agnes. Float a turd."

chapter 26

Today's a good day for Katie.

Her breathing tube stays coiled around the valve of her oxygen tank.

She's wearing knee-torn, ass-defining jeans. Nice bellybutton. She slips on her gray cross-country hoodie. The team logo, a sprinting cheetah, is on the front, and "Katie" is stamped on the back.

She stands before the mirror and slips the Beyoncé wig over her bald head. Adjusts it. Brushes the hair as if it were real. Teases the bangs. Puts on sugary lip-gloss. Brushes color onto her cheeks. Then she slips on some glasses and becomes Miss Hot Librarian.

Personally, I'd like to check out a book.

But it's time to go to work. She grabs her laptop, and we rush down the corridor.

"Hey, Yolanda. Hey, Robert."

She stops in every room. Everybody welcomes her.

She wants to know the most trivial stuff.

"Did you eat your sliced tomatoes?"

"Did you fill out that form?"

"Did you write that e-mail to your son? You want me to write it for you? Okay."

She bangs out the e-mail on her laptop, fires it off. Fast and easy. Like me, she believes in spontaneous writing. No pauses. Not even spell check. Done. Gone.

The old, nontechie residents are mildly shocked by the suddenness of her accomplishments. To have a burden lifted so quickly and easily. They beam their gratitude.

And she can't leave me out of it.

"Jonathan has a poem for you."

I read the rhyming crap from the Delphi library. Kipling. Longfellow. Whittier.

I bring my copy of *Leaves of Grass* and read Walt Whitman. I even read a few of my own.

Or . . .

"Phil, sing 'Danny Boy,' and Jonathan will play along."

We're standing in room 135. Phil's an amped-sales-exec-golfer type. Still has all his hair. He's been at the Delphi about sixteen weeks, same as me. At first, he had no time to be sick. Got dressed for work in his starched Nordstrom shirt and vintage slim-fit pants. Hair gel. Shiny tasseled shoes. But after a few days the tasseled shoes disappeared and the slippers came on. The hair gel disappeared. His shaving got sketchy—little islands of stubble appeared. Till finally he's just sitting here, in his bathrobe, watching the sky drip. The IV drip.

Katie's done some research. Knows Phil used to sing tenor in some glee club. Loves Irish and Scottish songs.

She pats his shoulder. "Hey, how does it go? 'Danny boy . . . something, something.'"

Phil clears his throat, warbles into gear:

"Oh Danny boy, the pipes, the pipes are calling."

I find it, key of C. Add the mellow seventh and the sadder shift from F to F minor. Phil lifts his voice. He does have a nice one, pure, like that opera singer Plácido Domingo. People slip into the room. Or watch from the doorway—the bed changer, the blood taker, the UPS guy. Phil hits it close enough so that we see visions of misty Ireland. Ruby strews mournful petals along the path.

When we stitch it up, everybody claps.

Phil's just warming up, though. He starts crooning "The Bonnie Banks o' Loch Lomond."

Death hangs over these Irish and Scottish songs. Just swap bagpipes and mountain heather for IV drips and hospital beds, and you have the Delphi.

Only here the pipes are flushing.

When we hit the chorus, Phil and I harmonize. He takes the high road. I take the low road.

Then he breaks into a song called "Whiskey in the Jar."

I strum it, fast and tappy.

Verse after verse. About thieves, sly women, and the "juice of the barley."

Phil and I crank the volume on the "Whack fal the daddy-o" chorus.

"Goddammit!" Phil says, slapping his knee.

Out in the corridor, Katie says, "That's the happiest I've ever seen him."

So now I'm the local troubadour.

Birdwell has taught us about the troubadours of old Europe who stood in cobbled village squares and sang of valorous kings and frolicking lovers. In those days, Birdwell said, the troubadour was the poet-historian who bound the daisies of the past into one bouquet for the peasants to sniff.

As Katie and I go from room to room, Ruby hanging from my neck, I begin to see myself as a "binder of daisies."

As titles go, I like it.

Ruby likes it, too. She no longer gasps for air in her gig bag.

If I sound any better these days, it's because of Ruby. Not me.

chapter 27

I'm sitting on a stool in a small house on a drippy hill in West Seattle. The owner doesn't give a damn about the upkeep of his house. Moss grows up one side and ivy down another.

But he gives a damn about music.

There's an upright piano in the living room, guitars and banjos on the wall, flutes, recorders, and hand drums scattered about. Even a triangle and a didjeridoo from Australia.

The owner of the house is Frank Conway, the unshaven, slouching man who one night got trapped in the vice of Mimi's tits, wandered home with her, rocked the house, and met me in the shadowy predawn hours of darkest winter.

"You gotta capture that every time," Frank says, meaning how I played "Here Comes the S-O-N." "That was core honesty, Jonathan. Just you and your gut. Wanna 'nother cup of coffee?"

I've already had two cups, but Frank's a big coffee drinker. Paraphernalia everywhere—mugs and spoons and filters and smells and stains. I'm thinking he needs to learn about taurine, because caffeine just doesn't do it.

"Yeah, sure," I say.

He limps into the kitchen on a sore heel. Fills our mugs, stirs in the powdered creamer. Limps back. His half-buttoned flannel shirt partially covers a V-neck T-shirt and small silver crucifix.

Everything about Frank Conway is an unmade bed. Sloppy

but comfortable. Unironed but hopeful. He's a grizzled Spring-steen, only without the spring in his step.

"The goal," he says, "is to play music only as *you* would play it. Not as I, or your brother, or Jimi Hendrix, would play it. It's all about you, Jonathan. Find that sweet spot inside yourself, forget the rest of the world, and you can coast all the way to Mexico."

He grabs his guitar. Fingerpicks the intro to "Crossing the River Styx." Clean and easy. Bends a note here and there. Starts to sing. His voice is strong coffee. Cream but no sugar.

It sounds a lot better than the original by Pinky Toe, at least to my ear. By pouring caffeine into it and cutting it with melancholy, he gives the song what it needs, heartache and muscle ache. He soaks it with the soreness of life.

"Listen, Jonathan, the middle part is easy—just strum it, your basic C–F–G–F chord pattern. You can do anything you want with that—play it straight or improvise. But the intro . . . those few, fast notes. Get 'em down, and when you've learned 'em, forget 'em. Your motor memory will keep you airborne, and you can fly wherever you want."

All of this makes sense to me. Like Yoda preaching to Luke. But there's a big difference between getting the theory down and the practice.

"Go on," Frank says, handing me his guitar. "Give it a try."

Frank's guitar is a Gibson Hummingbird acoustic. The caramel sound box has been chafed by years of play, but it's tonally bright and pure. That's the thing about guitars: Cheap ones full of laminate may shine on the outside, but they're dull on the inside. Time does not improve them. But those made of solid wood—spruce or maple or bubinga—are on an endless journey to perfection. They never stop getting better, even after the varnish has worn off. If you treat them well, that is.

Ruby's that way. She never stops getting better for me. Even with the extra fist-size hole in her sound box.

If only Ruby were a girl. She'd be tanned and sexy, shy and enlightened, a poet, an artist, but with some kind of injury, like a limp or an eye patch. Yeah, if Ruby were only a girl—that would solve a lot of my problems.

I grab a medium pick from the ashtray. Play a few arpeggios. Take a deep breath. Then I try the lick. After a few notes, I blow it. Start over. Blow it again.

This happens five or six more times.

"I hate this song!"

Frank nods. "Kind of like voting for Hitler, isn't it."

"But I like the way you play it."

"It's all about practice, Jonathan."

"What about the singing part?" I ask. "I can't hit those high notes. Not unless I squeeze my 'nads."

"Capo on the second fret," Frank says. "It's your best key. And practice with a metronome—do you have one?"

"Yeah, but it's broken."

He opens a drawer and tosses me a hand-size battery-powered metronome.

"Practice a thousand times, Jonathan. I'm not joking. A thousand times. Learn to play that intro exactly how Pinky Toe plays it. Once you've got it uploaded into your DNA, you can play it your own way. Don't try to break the rules till you've first mastered them. Then break 'em all you want."

"But how'm I gonna do all that in three weeks?"

"You're just gonna do it."

Frank reaches for his guitar, messes with some variations. Then he licks the tip of a pencil and jots some stuff into a notebook.

"Try this," he says, tearing out the page.

He's changed the arrangement. Some of the major chords have become minors or sevenths.

"Now it's more October," he says, "less July."

"Thanks," I say. "Can I use your bathroom?"

Frank's bathroom is full of unwashed coffee mugs and copies of the *Economist* magazine. He keeps a half-size Martin guitar on a stand by the toilet, within easy reach. On the wall is a poster depicting Abraham Lincoln swinging an ax, only the ax isn't really an ax, it's a Gibson Robot Flying V guitar. I take all this in while pissing.

"I didn't know Lincoln played," I say when I come back into the living room.

"Oh, he had the temperament of a great musician," Frank says. "A true voice, which he didn't change, though people pressured him to. That's what you gotta do, Jonathan, believe in your voice. The first time I heard you, man, you were bleeding inside. You've got the voice. You just gotta believe in yourself."

"Hey, I might get to play a Rickenbacker three-sixty six."

"*Whoa!*" Frank says. "That's as posh as it gets. George Harrison played a Ric. So did Jones of the Stones. McGuinn of the Byrds. Townshend of the Who. The list goes on and on. If any guitar defines sound as we know it, it's the Ric, especially the three-sixty series. Man, you'll be driving a Maserati."

"I might need racing gloves," I say.

Frank says, "How's your mom, Jonathan?"

"Oh, dude, she's crazy."

"She really gonna open a wedding chapel in your house?"

I nod. "That's the plan, anyway."

"And she's authorized and certified to do weddings and all that?"

"Yeah, she's got a divinity diploma."

"From where?"

"The mail."

Frank ponders this. "Well," he says, "all good ideas gotta start on the edge of something."

"Like the edge of sanity," I say.

Frank darkens. "Hey, man, don't crap on your mom. Remember, you lost a brother, but she lost a son."

Whoa! As far as I'm concerned, the lesson's over. I start to stand but get only as far as the edge of my stool.

What I want to say is, *He was my TWIN brother!* but Frank reads my mind.

"Jonathan, don't play that card. You're both holding the ace high."

"Ace of what?" I say. "Tragedy?"

"Exactly," he says, "the ace of tragedy. Maybe this wedding chapel idea isn't so crazy after all. Maybe it's on your mother's evolutionary road, just like poetry and music are on yours."

"Hey," I say, "between you and me, Mimi hasn't evolved all that much."

"You sure about that?"

I shrug, because I'm not sure—I'm not sure about anything.

"Jonathan, you ever try writing songs?"

"No."

"You being a poet and guitar player, it seems kind of a natural thing. Think on it."

"Yeah, I will."

"Keep in touch, Jonathan."

I fold the piece of paper with Frank's new arrangement and slip it into my shirt pocket.

"Thanks, man. Adios."

"Go with god, Jonathan."

chapter 28

I'm walking down the main hall at Taft, on my way to the Kenny G, when Mrs. Scranton rushes up.

"Oh, Jonathan, Dr. Jacobson wants you to have these."

She thrusts a manila envelope into my hands. I start to ask what's inside but stop myself. Anything from Gupti's gotta mean more work.

"Thanks," I say, and jam the envelope into my backpack.

Kyle grabs me by the arm and drags me down the hall.

"C'mon, dude," he says. "The crew is waiting."

The crew, as it turns out, is Javon on lights and Jordan on forklift. Nick has been appointed "guitar technician." And Kyle has brought in Ryan Lee, a soccer friend, for "security." This is necessary because of the extreme museum-worthiness of the Ric.

Kyle climbs on stage and bellows his plan: "Dudes, today we're gonna rehearse bringing the Velcro Kong out on stage, front and center, and lifting Jonathan into the paw."

He snaps his finger at Javon up in the control booth.

Javon hits some buttons and levers, and a giant hook starts rolling across the ceiling. It takes a couple of mouse-in-maze turns and stops above the Velcro Kong. Then the hook descends. Javon starts messing with the controls, trying to catch the hook on a metal loop on Kong's back. But he keeps missing. It's kind of like playing one of those fishing games at the arcade, only on a giant scale.

"Whoa, whoa, whoa!" Kyle shouts to Javon. "You gotta get it right, dude. We can't be taking an hour to get Kong out here."

This time, Javon scores. He jerks the Velcro Kong from the ancient shadows and pulls him out to center stage.

"Forklift!" Kyle shouts.

Jordan drives onto stage at the controls of a Clark forklift with balloon tires.

"Okay, dude," Kyle says to me. "You're on."

"What am I supposed to do?"

"Get up there," he says.

Jordan noses up in the forklift, plants the pallet at my feet.

"What about the Ric?" I ask.

"I'm not gonna risk using the Ric in rehearsals, man. We brought it out today to get used to it. You know, air it out and sort of get over that star thing it has."

Kyle turns to Nick and Ryan, who stand like sentinels on both sides of the Ric.

"Dudes, show us Ricky."

Nick snaps open the silver case. Lifts the cherry prince out of his velvet bed. Ryan bows before it.

"Just pretend you've got the Ric strapped on," Kyle says.

I step on the pallet, and Jordan starts cranking. He jacks me about as high as the third shelf at Costco. Of course, the stage, too, is pretty high. The combination of heights sucks the air out of me.

"Whoa!" I say. "What's the word for fear of heights?"

"Halitosis," Ryan says.

"Shouldn't I at least have a safety line?" I ask.

"Dude, this is *theater vérité*," Kyle says. "But that reminds me, we'll need a safety line for the Ric."

"The Ric!"

"Don't be a pussy, man. Now jump into Kong's paw."

Stepping from the fork into Kong's hand means letting go of my hold and straddling nothing but air. The only way to do this is quickly, with a little jump and without thinking about it.

God knows how I'll manage it with the Ric strapped on.

I leap into Kong's hand, and as I do, my weight throws him. He begins to lean like a tree. A panicky cackle rises from the stage. Kyle, Nick, and Ryan rush to Kong's knees to shore him up.

Now I'm huddled in the cupped hand of the Velcro Kong. Clouds of butterflies swarm through my gut tubes. A few flutter up to my throat. If I feel this way now, how'm I gonna feel on Friday, June 1, when I stand here facing twelve hundred people?

"Hey, Jonathan," Kyle says. "We got balance issues down here. One of Kong's feet is shorter than the other."

I peer down. "How did that happen?"

Fact is, by jerking Kong from his petrified place in the shadows, Javon has ripped off the sole of one foot, including Kong's gorilla toes.

The crew inspects the damaged foot. In the end, Kyle says, "Just don't lean too far to the side, dude. Stay centered. Everything'll be cool."

Jordan lowers me to the stage, and we go through the setup three more times. Kyle and Javon work out the lighting. Now it's all science. We can hook and roll Kong from behind the curtain and get me into the hand in just under ninety seconds, with Javon capturing me in a circle of blinding silver light.

Just as long as I stay in the center of Kong's cupped hand, I'm fine.

"Great rehearsal, dudes," Kyle says. "Nick, look at getting a wireless mike for Jonathan. Ryan, work on getting a safety line set up for the Ric. I'll get the jazz band to play 'Pick Up the Pieces' while we set up."

Everybody's looking at me, as if I might have something to say.

And I do.

"There's one thing we didn't rehearse," I say.

"What's that, dude?"

"The song."

"Oh, yeah," Kyle says. "I knew we forgot something. Well, just practice on your own."

He looks pleased. His part of the show is coming together. Mine is crashing and burning.

chapter 29

A dozen oxygen bottles stand by the door in David Cosgrove's room. "My empties," he calls them.

His teeth—*whoa!* He truly, desperately needs to brush them. One of the uppers has come loose, flaps like a pet door.

From a distance, his complexion is tanned. Close up, it's blotchy and veiny. A road map with lots of purple and red highways.

Caregivers come and go. Bring pills. Crackers. Pineapple juice. Roll David on his side, change his sheets. One caregiver is Nigerian. Two are Ethiopian. A doctor—who is not African but of the short, stocky, pink-white North American variety—enters the room.

"Are you in pain, David?"

"No."

"Is there anything you need?"

"I could use a blowjob."

We laugh. Three guys. Three generations. One timeless thought.

The doctor leaves. Time to board the USS *Gabriel Trask*.

"Where were we, sailor?"

"Down below," I say. "Trying to keep the ship from sinking."

"Oh, yes," he says. "We were trying to stay afloat long enough to reach Kerama Retto. We kept those submersible pumps humming."

He fumbles with his breathing tube. I set down my writing pad and go to his bedside. Untangle the tube.

"Thank you, Jonathan. I'm embarrassed to say I've already forgotten—"

"Manning the submersible pumps," I say.

"Oh, yes. Down below, there was no difference between day and night. But I know from the official report that it was evening, nearly dark."

"Yeah," I say. "Something like nineteen hundred hours."

David nods. "We'd entered a channel between two small islands. Were in about ten fathoms of water, within sight of the harbor at Kerama Retto. By now, we'd won the battle to save the ship; at least, we thought so. What we didn't know was that an enemy sub was stalking us. Just when we thought we were okay, that our war was over, that's when it happened."

"That's when it always happens," I say.

"Yes, Jonathan. It would seem so."

"Wasn't it, like, a perfect hit?"

"Textbook," David says. "The torpedo slammed into us amidships and detonated our ammo magazines. Everything blew."

"*Whoa!*" I say. "Give me some details."

David rallies his memory. "Most of all, I remember the horrific shudder. A convulsion of everything around and within."

"Hey," I say, "this may sound weird, but I know how you felt."

"Yes, Jonathan. And I know how you felt."

I sense he does. Unlike everybody else who says he knows— David *does* know how I felt, or at least comes close. "A convulsion of everything around and within." That basically sums up my past year. David's and my lives are a gazillion miles apart.

Two leafless trees standing at opposite ends of the desert. But now the spheres align; our shadows stretch out and touch.

I say, "You got some kind of gash, right?"

"Yes, see here."

He traces a scar that runs up his temple and across his forehead.

I step out of the chair, lean close. Check out the scar. It's kind of hidden because of all the wrinkles and creases. But when he was younger, it must have stood out. A jagged reminder.

"All of us got banged up, Jonathan. Not one of us was spared by that explosion. I've never been ashamed of this scar. Never tried to hide it."

"Was it dark?"

"Yes. As our engines died, and the propellers stopped churning, our lights went out. An emergency lamp came on, and then it, too, dimmed and died."

"Black dungeon dark?"

"Yes, Jonathan. Not a shimmer of light."

David sips his pineapple juice. Winces at the tartness.

"How long did it take you to sink?"

"No time at all," he says. "Imagine a seesaw when a plump child sits on one end. Well, that was our ship. As the stern filled with water, the bow rode up, and we slid into the ocean. It happened very fast. Amid deafening noise—imploding metal, whooshing cataracts of water, then, finally, eerie metallic groans. The sea boiled up around us. To our waist, then up to our shoulders. I had no doubt I was a goner."

"How does that feel?" I ask. "I mean, how does it feel to know you're gonna die?"

David opens his mouth to speak but can't. Everything clashes on his face. All the years and memories, the gut reflex to be stoic, the wanting to talk. It's all there. But he can't say it. He shakes his head.

"How deep is ten fathoms?" I ask.

"Sixty feet."

"And you still had air?"

"Yes, barely. We'd settled on the bottom in such a way as to trap air."

"Hey," I say, "I'm in a dark place myself. Nothing like being boxed under water, but it feels like it."

David nods, comes back into the present. "My vocal chords need a rest, Jonathan. Why don't you tell me about it."

"Nothing to tell, just . . ."

"Yes?"

"I know what you've been through."

"It's all the same, Jonathan. Armageddon is Armageddon."

"For me," I say, "it's like a tightness in my throat. It's like choking."

"Share it, Jonathan. It'll get better."

"So far," I say, "it only gets worse."

David struggles with his breathing tube.

"How's your oxygen, dude?"

"Running low, I'm afraid."

I grab a fresh bottle from the foot of the bed. Plug him in. Watch his chest rise and fall.

By now, the canary yellow legal pad is jammed with my scrawlings, scratchings, and doodles. I stuff it into my backpack. Grab a new pad from the drawer. Settle back in my chair.

David looks wiped out. I expect him to tell me to leave, though I hope he won't. He waves a finger.

"Fire up the boilers, Jonathan."

"Already fired up."

He takes a deep breath. Actually, he takes little sips of air that total a deep breath.

"*Anoxia,*" he says, "means an extreme lack of oxygen. This is how we would die, starved for air."

David looks at me in his blindness. Seems to see me.

"Before I tell you, Jonathan, I want you to know—I've told this only once before, to Navy interrogators at the inquest. That was decades and decades ago. And they asked only factual questions, which I answered factually, as one does before a Navy board of inquiry. They did not ask for more. For example, they did not ask what the event meant to me or, at a profoundly human level, how it changed me. And in those days, I tried not to reflect on the experience. Or plumb its depths. Quite the contrary, I wanted to build a wall between me and my memories. But you get to a point, Jonathan, when sealing it off just arrests everything in your life. I should have talked about this long ago. We all need to be heard, Jonathan, if only by one other human being. We need to talk about our Armageddons. I feel a great need to talk about mine now."

"Well," I say, "you're in luck, because today just happens to be Open Armageddon Day."

"How fortuitous," David says. He takes a sip of oxygen. "Now, where were we?"

"Ten fathoms deep in the black dungeon dark."

"Oh, yes," he says. "I'd call out a name, and each man would say a few words, very much with the awareness that . . . that we were—"

"Doomed," I say.

"Yes," David says. "What each man had to say, Jonathan, well, you don't think you'll ever have to say, or at least not until you're a helluva lot older. We were young men."

"Can you remember any of those words?"

"Not verbatim. But I remember the spirit of them. They boiled down to the same thing. Cherish life."

"Everybody said that—cherish life?"

"Each in his own way, yes."

The door opens and one of David's caregivers walks in. She's Ethiopian, a slim, pouty beauty. Dress her in clingy satin, slap her on the cover of *Vogue*—she'd sell a million copies. Instead, she's wearing smocky hospital clothes. Carrying a tray with a pill cup on it. No wonder she looks depressed.

"Leave us!" David shouts.

Somehow, in his frailty, his voice booms.

The Ethiopian beauty freezes. Her *Vogue* eyes widen.

"You better leave," I say.

She retreats into the corridor, muttering some dialect.

"Poor girl," David says. "I was hard on her."

"I doubt she'll go to your funeral now," I say.

David grins. "I'll make amends later. Now, where were we?"

"Sitting on the bottom of the ocean cherishing life."

"Oh, yes," David says. "I must've drifted off, because I remember opening my eyes and seeing the face of the man next to me—a gray death mask—and thinking, *This is it, this is what it is.* Then realizing—*My god! I can see him.* And yes, there was light, very faint, a shimmer coming in. *My god, light! How could it be?* Well, we'd made it through the night, and now day-light was filtering through the broken hull where the torpedo had hit. All I saw was a thin shimmer deep in the flooded passageway.

"I shook the man, Terry McClendon, a helluva gunner, a big, good man from Wink, Texas, and he saw for himself. Perked right up. 'Don't rouse them,' I said. 'Not yet.'

"I ducked under water and swam toward the light. In moments my lungs were bursting. It was too far, too deep. I turned back.

"We roused the men, and they saw for themselves. A couple were too weak to swim, but most were simply too afraid to try. One or two did try and got no farther than I, but most, well, it was choose your poison, and they would rather suffocate slowly than drown. Here we were, with a chance, if only a slim one, and they were choosing to stay put."

"You'd think they'd try," I say. "Especially after all that talk about cherishing life."

"People don't always follow their own wisdom, Jonathan."

"So what happened?"

"I told them, 'I'm going again, and if I reach the opening, I'll bang my knife three times. Like this.' And I slid out my knife and pounded the hilt against the steel bulkhead three times, below the water line. The sound resonated. Clearly. Then I lay my head on my arm and took air into my lungs. Slowly and methodically. I looked at them one last time—the light had grown brighter—and slid under water.

"I swam toward that shimmer, Jonathan. In a matter of sec-onds, I was dying for air. And there was an instant . . . and then I was beyond the point of turning back. Behind me was all darkness. I focused on that shimmer, let it draw me. Getting closer, I could see clouds of plankton and the deep greenish-blue of the ocean. A calm came over me. A peace. Whether I'd live or die, I knew I'd made the right choice."

"Hey," I say, "where I'm sitting, you did."

David says, "The light showed a great gash in the side of the ship, a mass of tangled steel where the torpedo had struck. I took my knife and pounded three times. Then I squeezed through. Swam out, dropping the knife, every last atom of me starved for air, and shot toward the surface, which seemed forever above me.

"When I broke through, I filled my lungs. Drank deeply all the air they could hold. I couldn't get enough. I wanted to drink the whole damn sky. My ears were bleeding, my nose was bleeding. I had a monster-size headache and was swallowing blood. God knows what nitrous poisons I'd set loose in my body by coming up so fast. But I was alive."

"Yeah," I say. "You sure were."

"Life is a beautiful thing, Jonathan."

"So what happened?"

"I glanced about and saw the harbor at Kerama Retto—no more than a couple miles away. When I blinked and got my eyes right, I could see the silhouettes of naval vessels—destroyers, tenders, liberty ships—at anchor.

"I hovered there, waiting for my men to follow.

"Ducking under, I saw my ship—the *Gabe*, number four fourteen—on which I'd lived and served for three years. The top of the mast was only a fathom or two beneath me. The ship itself was a massive blurry shadow.

"I surfaced. 'C'mon,' I shouted. 'C'mon!'

"Jonathan, all the joy of being alive was gone, because no one else followed."

"Or," I say, "they tried but they couldn't make it."

"Some did try, Jonathan. That's the victory. You've got to try. Come here."

I set down my legal pad and go to his bed.

"Give me your hand, Jonathan."

I hold out my hand, as if to shake, and he clasps it. Wraps mine in both of his.

"We'll take a moment," David says. "If we were at sea, we would toss a wreath, as an homage. Just a moment of silence, Jonathan. For everyone we care about whom we've lost. They will never be with us again, but we won't forget them. I'd like to include your brother in this."

"Yeah," I say. "He'd like that."

David's hand is soft and frail. It's like I can feel all of his illnesses through it. The tangle of old age, weak veins, and cancer cells.

His lips move. He speaks some kind of prayer, and I see Telly as I often do, flying on his long board.

Happy to be alive.

Chosen for life.

Impossibly dead.

When I open my eyes, David is staring at me.

"You must remember, Jonathan: Point yourself toward that shimmer. And keep going—always keep going."

He lets go. I sit down.

"So how'd you get back?"

David gropes for the box of Kleenex. Pulls out a tissue. Blasts his nose.

"I started swimming. After a while, I got picked up by a launch combing through the debris. They took me to the make-shift hospital at Kerama Retto."

"Couldn't they send down divers?"

"Oh, they did, Jonathan. But it took hours to organize that dive." He shakes his head. "You see, there was really only that one chance."

"And some tried to get out?"

"Yes."

"How do you know that? Did they find bodies floating in the passageway?"

"Yes, Jonathan."

"Hey," I say, "don't blame yourself."

"I don't," David says. "Neither should you."

"Me?"

"Now, I'm afraid I've run out of steam."

David closes his eyes. Leans back, exhausted. I slip my legal pad into my backpack.

"Thanks," I say.

"No, thank *you,* Jonathan."

chapter 30

It's way past midnight. I'm standing in my room twirling a lariat. Actually, it's just an old clothesline—and it's not much of a twirl, either.

I try to lasso my desk. I widen the loop, and eventually it lands just right, hooked at the base of a great mountain of books and notebooks and empty Red Bull cans and flung T-shirts and stacks and mounds of everything else.

I tug, and slowly this great mountain slides to the brink of my desk. I jerk, and it plunges over the edge into the canyon below. An end-of-world event. Armageddon.

Yippee-aye-oh-cuy-ay!

I take a sock and wipe the dust and grit off the surface of my desk. For the first time in history, it's clean.

I open my backpack and shake the contents onto my desk. Out fall about twenty canary yellow legal pads, the pages all feathery and fluffy from hard note taking.

Last to shake out is a manila envelope—the one Mrs. Scranton handed me in the hall at Taft.

I'd forgotten all about it.

I tear it open. On official stationery—"Gupti R. Jacobson, PhD, Principal, William Howard Taft High School"—is a note in the fine hand of multiarmed Shiva:

Jonathan,
Thought you might like these.

"These" are a stack of formal invitations to the graduation exercises on Friday, June 1—two weeks from today. Normally they go to graduating seniors, but I'm an exception because . . .

I'M ON THE PROGRAM!

Gupti has enclosed a draft of the program. My spot comes at the end. Gupti herself will introduce me.

I'm listed by name and these words:

Performing "Crossing the River Styx" (Pinky Toe)

I fling the invitations at the wall. Down they flutter. Like shot doves.

From various other stashes—mostly Ruby's gig bag—I build a tower of legal pads. Yellow and rectangular. Thirty-six pads jammed with my barely legible scrawl, scratchings, and doodlings.

Countless words.

The raw materials from which I must build the story of David O. H. Cosgrove II's life.

I open a twelve-pack of taurine (8.3-ounce cans, sugarized), platoon the cans at the far corner of my desk. Post my bottle of maximum strength NoDoz at the head of the platoon, the bulky sergeant. Position my laptop. Adjust the light.

I pull Ruby's rocking chair over next to me. She can keep me company. Lift me over any humps and hurdles.

These are the essential tools of the writing trade: notes, laptop, taurine, NoDoz, guitar.

If only I had a candle to invite the muse. *Whoa!* I run downstairs, dig through a kitchen drawer, find a dildo-shaped Christmas candle.

Upstairs, I light it.

Now I stare at the empty screen. Words . . . do not appear. They hide in prairie dog holes.

My mind is mud.

After a while, my eyes start to droop. Drowsiness creeps in.

I jerk awake. Pop three NoDoz. Peel open a can and bull down 8.3 ounces of taurine. This little cocktail kicks me in the head.

So where's my muse? When will she land on my shoulder? Whisper in my ear that first sentence? One sentence to start the snowball rolling down the slope. Start the prairie dog barking.

I reach for Ruby. Crunch some twelve-bar blues. Brocade them with pinkie sevenths.

Since I'm into it, I place Frank's metronome on my desk and try the intro to "Crossing the River Styx." Play it straight through. I still can't keep up with Pinky Toe, but I'm getting better. As for the singing, Frank Conway is right. Everything sort of falls into place when I clamp the capo on the second fret.

I play the intro till I can't stand it any longer. Then I fall into my punkie meditation ditty—my Telly tune, sweet and complex, strawberry dipped in vinegar.

Ruby sounds warm and forgiving. When I play her, I don't know if I'm making music, praying, or wasting time. But she makes me feel better. Ruby always makes me feel better. There are times when I think she's my girlfriend, and times when she's more like a grandmother, because there are no complications. Just flat-out unconditional love.

I set Ruby back in her rocking chair. Slip my North Face vest over her to keep her warm. Grab a stack of legal pads and riffle through them. My eye catches on this quote:

"Maybe we don't need to hit the duck. Maybe all we need to do is say what we must say once, to another human being, openly and honestly, with humility and remorse. Maybe that is enough."

I type these words. They become the first sentences of my book.

The first sentences of the story of David Cosgrove's life.

Finally, the snowball has started to roll.

The prairie dog has poked out of his hole.

And barked.

• • •

I work all night. It gets so cold through my leaky window, I put on two hoodies.

Now it's Saturday morning. Punch-your-pockets drizzly.

Typical spring day in Seattle.

My back feels gnarled. My butt bone throbs. But I don't care because I have flown. During the night, I have jumped off the precipice, spread my wings, and swooped. I have smashed rules—of spelling, punctuation, and syntax. Gleefully. I have flown fast and far.

I view the doc in print mode—thirty-four pages. Click on word count: 9,322.

Jeezus!

Not even Charles Bukowski—Uncle Buk—wrote that fast.

I consider going for an even ten thousand words, but that would be quantity over quality. Besides, I'll get back to it tonight. I can hardly wait.

Writing, in the zone, is about the best feeling ever.

I'm way past writing for the fun of it. Lots of times it's not fun. I write because I have to.

If Stalin or Hitler arrested me and tossed me into one of those camps, I would carve words with my fingernails. If they cut off my fingers, I would write with my teeth. If they pulled out my teeth, I would blink my words to any listening bird. If they cut off my eyelids, I would fart code into the troposphere.

You'd have to kill me to stop me from writing.

It's how I breathe.

• • •

I go down to the kitchen, build a massive bowl of Special K. Slice a banana on top. Blanket the surface with C&H pure cane sugar from Hawaii.

Mimi's stuck a note on the fridge: "Where's my ad?"

Oh, yeah. The *West Seattle Herald* ad I was supposed to write. Forgot about that.

Because I'm still in the zone, I grab a sheet of paper from Mimi's printer. Mess with a few ideas. The C&H kicks in, and I write:

"Believe in Love Again."
The Chapel of the Highest Happiness
Where Dream Weddings Come True
Opening June 1
in the Heart of West Seattle's
Historic Delridge Neighborhood
Rev. Miriam Jones officiating

My phone burps. Nick.

"Get your ass over here, dude!" I say.

"Aye, aye, captain," Nick says.

It's primer day. Armed with extra-wide brushes and iPods, Nick and I paint a coat of white on two sides of the house. Dismantling and rebuilding the scaffolding.

At about three p.m., Javon shows up in new shoes—Zoom LeBron VIs. "Hell no, I'm not paintin' nothin'," he says. But I'm paying, so he borrows a pair of my splattered Dunk Lows.

We attack the remaining two sides of the house. Swap iPods to keep it fresh. All agree, Jason Mraz sucks to paint by, but Afroman makes the scaffold bounce. I'm introducing my thicks to taurine, and today we have the strength of charging bulls. We are constantly refreshed and stimulated. Maximally efficient.

We're high up on the scaffolding, slapping away, when Mimi comes out to inspect. Naturally, she's forgotten to button the top half of her blouse, so the inspection works both ways. But I don't care. Today, as long as my team is happy, they can do anything they want.

"Hey," she shouts, "where's my ad?"

I reach into my pocket, fold the sheet of paper into an airplane, and fling it. It nosedives onto the grass.

Mimi bends over, torques, picks up the little plane. She flattens the wings, ponders the words.

Bursts into a smile.

She digs into her tits and finds some cash, shouts: "You've earned this, baby!"

She anchors the bills under a paintbrush handle.

Then she thrusts a fist at the sky. "Go, boys!"

We go and go till the light is gone at ten p.m. By then, we're done. The house is fully primed. We've even slapped the first coat of purple on the south side. Nick, Javon, and I stand on the sidewalk and bask in the glory of our work.

Javon is so greasy, he doesn't want to touch his spotless Zoom LeBron VIs. He hooks a hanger onto the heels and drops them delicately into a grocery bag. Then he and Nick cash out—I'm a generous boss—and slouch into the dark.

Day is done. Gone the sun. Come the muse.

Time to start writing again.

chapter 31

I'm in the mystical trough. A valley where demons and angels dance. A place of writing frenzy. Think Jack Kerouac, man of roads and wine. Think Charles Bukowski, man of apartments and wine.

Think me, man of taurine and NoDoz.

We are writers of the mystical trough—most alive in the after-midnight hours.

Those writers who no longer feel the pain went to bed a long time ago. They find relief in sleep.

I find relief in the mystical trough. My fingers fly across the keyboard.

Click, click, click, click.

In telling the story of David Cosgrove, everything is darkened by the fate of those men under water, trapped in the sunken USS *Gabriel Trask* off Kerama Retto in April 1945.

When I write about David's ice hockey days or the death of his dog, Gil, or his first "unofficial girlfriend," Blue Feather Chang, I'm thinking about those men under water.

I see their shadowy images in all aspects of David's life. They seem very much at home in my own head, too. My mind is a fertile place for shadows to grow.

My phone has been burping half the night, but I've ignored it. Then one prolonged *brrraacckkk* breaks my spell. I reach over to check the number, pretty sure it's just one of my insomniacal thicks.

I see the name "Katie" on my screen.

Jerk thumb. Catch the call.

"Were you asleep?"

"I never sleep."

"Jonathan, David died."

• • •

The first bus uptown leaves at 4:55 a.m., and I'm on it. So is a baker's dozen of early risers and all nighters. They are like the light in the sky—scales of night and day, weary and fresh, beer and soap.

An old woman with a big suitcase and terrible dermatitis on her hands climbs on. I pray she won't sit beside me. She does, of course. Her suitcase takes up half the aisle. She tries to make small talk with me. Fails.

At the West Seattle Junction, she gets up, struggles with her suitcase. It pains her to lift it. I grab the handle and carry the suitcase off the bus. Plant it beside her. "Thank you, dear," she says. "Whatever's troubling you, don't give up."

Jeezus, is it that obvious?

I transfer to the 128. The rest of the way up California Avenue, I'm zoned out. The world blurs by.

When I glance across the aisle, Telly is sitting there. Long blond hair. Yellow T-shirt. Gazing ahead. Unaware of me.

It's like Abe Lincoln has swung his ax and cut a gash in the sun. The golden morning bleeds sadness.

Partly, my thoughts are the culmination of everything, made raw all over again. And partly they're because the taurine and NoDoz are wearing off. I'm starting to see halos.

Walking the last blocks to the Delphi, I stop on the bridge over Schmitz Park. It's a long ways down to the creek, still sleeping in the morning shadows. Down there where a handful of Telly lives, mingling with memories of Grandpa. I could easily climb onto the guardrail. It's very tempting.

I keep walking.

At the Delphi, the early risers sit in the TV lounge watching the early bird news. Flat Ass, at the reception desk, catches my eye. Gestures for me to sit and wait.

So I sit in the TV lounge, alone in the corner. Point my body away from the news. Grab a magazine, *Wise Traveler.* Flip though it. Barely looking. Just riffling.

My eye trips on an ad, a little rectangle of blue. It shows a tanned lady in a white bikini standing knee-deep in the ocean. Behind her the sea tapers away and melts into the sky.

In coconut-brown letters just above her golden left shoulder are these words:

Adios, Nirvana!

I see all this in a blink—in the tenth of a second it takes to riffle a page.

As I keep riffling, something begins to gnaw at me. A revelation can be like that—a rat gnawing an electric wire. The rat keeps gnawing till finally it chomps through and . . .

ZAP!

YE-EOWWW!

Finally, here are the words.

All my feelings sardine-packed into six syllables, and they aren't even English:

A-di-os, Nir-va-na.

Goodbye to . . . bliss . . . and happiness.

Because that's what Nirvana is, I think.

And love and beauty and hope.

Stuff I'm always searching for when I write my poems.

Or play Ruby.

Yeah! I think. *Somebody gets it—somebody* finally *gets it.*

But when I flip back to the lady in the white bikini, practically sweating with excitement, I'm shocked again. My eyes—my careless, dyslexic eyes—have tricked me.

The little blue rectangle that seemed to say everything now says nothing.

The actual words are these:

Adios, Havana!

Goodbye, capital city of Cuba.

Goodbye, salsa and tortillas.

Goodbye, Fidel and Raúl Castro.

Then I realize that my eyes—my visionary eyes—have stumbled onto a phrase all my own. And not just any phrase—a code, a password, a philosophy for life.

All rolled into one fat cigar.

One two-word poem that says everything.

The ultimate poem.

I stand and face all the early risers sitting in the TV lounge. Those hooked to oxygen tanks. Those in wheelchairs. The blank. The bald. The bland. The dying. The denying.

And I shout:

"ADIOS, NIRVANA!"

Flat Ass rushes over and grabs my arm. She walks me to David's room. Knocks. Katie answers. She's wearing no wig today. Bald as a Ping-Pong ball.

Gary Death is here, too. Pink faced. Smelling of cigarettes. "Just about done," he says.

He's brought his metal suitcase. Unfolded it into a gurney. Zipped David into a gray bag.

"Would you like to see him?"

"Yeah."

Gary unzips the bag. Now I can see David's face.

There are many kinds of stillness. One is the stillness of sleep, and one is the stillness of death. The inside of David's mouth is black.

Katie wraps her arms around me. Hugs me tightly.

I feel the warmth of her body through my coat.

I feel her thinness. Her disease. Her breasts. Her strength.

I close my eyes and see David swimming toward that shimmer. See him bursting through the surface of the ocean and drinking all that sky.

Katie is shaking. Or maybe it's me. I can't tell.

"Shh," she says.

"Hey, can somebody get the door?" Gary asks.

"Yeah, yeah," I say, jumping to the door.

I hold it open, and Gary rolls out, pushing the gurney with David all zipped up.

As we wheel down the corridor into the lobby, David is king. Respected by all. Not with trumpets and bows, but with straightened posture, a universal twitching awareness of our mortality.

Everybody's wondering, how can I arrange the daisies and dandelions of my life into a better bouquet?

The answer is, you can't.

Life is random.

Life is absurd.

Life is deadly.

The bouquet arranges itself.

And it doesn't always bloom or smell good.

Katie and I follow the gurney out the side entrance into the parking lot. Gary opens the back door of the van and rams the gurney into the fender. *Bang*—presto! The gurney is now folded neatly into a metal suitcase again. David is resting peacefully on a platform in back.

Gary starts to shut the door.

"Wait!"

I reach into my coat pocket and pull out an invitation to the Taft graduation ceremony on June 1.

I unzip the bag a few inches and slip the envelope inside. Zip it up.

"Hope you can make it, dude," I say.

"And you, too," I say, handing an invitation to Katie. "And this one's for Agnes."

I hand another invitation to Gary Death.

He reads it. "'Crossing the River Styx'—*whew!*"

Katie blows a kiss. "Bye-bye, David."

And I whisper, "Adios."

chapter 32

It's days later. My room is jammed with thicks. Kyle, Javon, Nick, Jordan. Ryan Lee is here, too.

They sprawl on my floor. Sit at my desk. Mess on my laptop. Flip the channels on my TV. What's mine is theirs. And vice versa. It's the law of thickness.

My only rule—treat Ruby with respect. And they do. She sits among us, royal in her rocking chair, the best chair in the room.

Used to be, I shared this chaos with Telly, and everyone wandered back and forth across the hall, between our rooms. But now, of course, Telly's door is shut. Sealed. His room a shrine.

They steal glances in that direction. Though he may be gone, his soul is still there. We all feel it.

Jordan goes down to the kitchen, returns with platefuls of microwaved burritos and tater tots, a bottle of ketchup tucked under his arm. The plates go around. Even though the tots were supposed to be baked, not microwaved, they are spongily, saltily delicious. Gone in thirty seconds. Basically inhaled.

The burritos last about forty-five seconds.

Now Kyle goes down to the kitchen, returns with a giant plastic bag filled with Mimi's frozen grapes.

"Aha!" Ryan Lee says.

"Dudes," Kyle says, "I think we all need some one hundred–

proof antioxidants. You know, to fight daily stress and delay the aging process. These grapes were personally hand selected and injected by the finest MILF in West Seattle."

"Respect!" Nick says.

But Kyle can't shut up.

". . . who I personally asked out on a date tonight, but wouldn't you know it, some greasy, broken-down dick-face beat me to it. She could've had ME!"

I pitch a frozen grape at Kyle. It bounces off his head.

Suddenly, the air is filled with frozen grapes and open orifices. We follow Kyle and Javon out into the hallway, where they demonstrate their finesse. Javon pitches to Kyle—fastball grapes, knuckle ball grapes, curve ball grapes. Kyle anticipates every pitch, catches nearly every one in his mouth.

When the grapes are all gone—packed safely in our bellies, where they begin to ferment—we tumble back into my room.

"Shut up, dudes," Kyle says. "Now that we've had our feast, and our fun, it's time to get down to business."

Everybody slides or slouches or rolls till a ragged circle is formed. I sit on my bed, above and a little apart.

"Dogs of West Seattle," Kyle says, "lend me your ears. This time tomorrow, we will have made history at Taft High School."

He frames an imaginary neon marquee: "Starring Jonathan and the Velcro Kong!"

Everybody grins.

I say, "This time tomorrow, we will *be* history."

"Dudes," Kyle says, "prepare yourselves, cuz we're gonna be celebrities. Everybody—parents, teachers, siblings, even grandmothers—will be talking about us. They will tune in to the six o'clock news, but the real news will be the Velcro Kong and

Jonathan. And, of course, me and Javon, in a slightly more intellectual way, as theater artists. But actually all of us, cuz after all, we are *one,* are we not? *Thick,* are we not?"

"Thick as a brick at the end of a stick," Jordan says.

"Been together since preschool, have we not?" Kyle says.

"Not me," Ryan says. "I didn't know any of you dudes till eighth grade."

"Be humble," Kyle says, ignoring Ryan. "That's our motto. We fly the flag of dude humility."

"Dude humility!" we chant.

Kyle crunches his fist and farts. It's a form of both punctuation and exclamation.

"Phew, man!" Jordan says, fanning the air. "Too much grease."

"And don't forget," Kyle says. "We're here because of, and for, our man Jonathan."

They all turn. The soul of Telly has entered the room. They look at me, but they see Telly.

"Yeah, don't forget that," I say. "And remember to be humble."

"Yep, yep," Kyle says. "Tomorrow at this time, our man Jonathan will be free and clear with Gupti. He will have paid his debt to society with a simple song by a band called . . . What's that name, again?"

"Pinky Toe," Nick says.

Javon says, "Hey, you got that song all worked out?"

I shrug.

"You wanna practice it for us?" he asks.

"Hell, no," I say.

"Man," Javon says, "to be both honest *and* humble, you look like shit."

I say, "And you look like a pit bull with your grandmother's face transplanted onto it."

"Dudes!" Kyle says. "Peace."

I reach for a can of taurine.

Kyle catches my wrist. "No, no, no," he says. "Tonight, you're gonna sleep the sleep of a baby. Pampered and powdered. And to make sure of it . . ."

He fishes a bottle of pills from his pocket.

"Say hello to your new nighttime friends," he says. "They are gentle, fast-acting, and extremely potent."

He shakes out a pill. Holds it between his thumb and forefinger. "This here is Angelina Jolie whispering love songs into Jonathan's left ear. And this"—he holds up another pill—"is whoever Jonathan wants it to be, Carrie Underwood or Pamela Anderson or—"

"Or all the Pussycat Dolls mud wrestling," Ryan says.

Nick shakes his head. "Nah. For Jonathan, it's gotta be, like, the elf queen in Lord of the Rings. Or some Celtic poetess."

Kyle nods. "Yeah, yeah, this one's a Celtic poetess whispering in Jonathan's right ear."

"And she shops at Victoria's Secret," Jordan says.

"Dudes!" I say. "You *do* know me."

Nick grabs Ruby from the rocking chair, flops beside me. Lets me see the worry in his eyes.

"Know what I want?" Nick says.

"No idea, man."

He slips Ruby into my arms. "To get loud again."

There's a chorus of *yeah*s.

Well, hell, I'm not exactly in a musical mood, but Ruby's part of me and my hands feel good on her neck and shapely body. And the grapes make it easier.

"Hey, why not."

I tune on five. The strings are getting black. If I were a better friend to Ruby, I'd invest in some new strings, maybe even splurge on Martin Extended Lifes. But I like the way she sounds on old strings. More like a sexy mom than a sexy daughter. Old strings give Ruby a far-from-virgin tonality. A quiet, sensual maturity.

While I'm tuning and chiming, Nick leaves the room. I expect to hear the bathroom door open and him pissing, but instead I hear the old familiar creak of Telly's door opening. I stop tuning. Stand. Peer into the hall. The light is on in Telly's room. Nick comes out carrying two of Telly's guitars.

"What're you doin', man?" I say.

Nick hands Telly's Fender electric to Jordan and his Thunderbird bass to Kyle.

"Hey," I say. "Didn't you hear me?"

Nick pivots and goes back into Telly's room.

"Guess not," Kyle says.

Now Nick comes out with Telly's Harmony acoustic and a set of drumsticks.

He hands the drumsticks to Ryan and the acoustic to Javon.

A quiet descends on us. In my mind, I'm angry, but I don't feel angry. What Nick's doing is a violation, but it doesn't feel wrong. We watch him the way you watch a minister breaking bread at church. Under a spell.

Now he's back with Telly's two amplifiers and a distortion

pedal. Everybody's untangling cables, heaving my books and dirty shirts aside, plugging in.

Except me. I stand there, paralyzed. In the past year, no one, except Mimi and me, has set foot in Telly's room. But Nick has just done it. Broken the invisible seal. Walked right in. He shoves his face in mine. "Don't you think it's time?"

If anybody else said that, I might explode. But it's Nick talking. So I let it sink in. And what he's just done feels right. Not in my head, but in my cells.

"Dude," Kyle says in a loud voice. "How 'bout that song 'Nature Is a Whore'?"

"It's called 'In Bloom,'" I say.

"Well, whatever it's called, let's do it."

Kyle was born with percussive hands. He passes the bass to Ryan in exchange for the drumsticks. Javon plays a better bass than acoustic, swaps with Ryan. Jordan would rather play harmonica, rummages in my desk for my Hohner blues beginner kit, tests a chrome back, key of G. Only then does he yield the Fender electric to Nick. But Nick can't tune a guitar, so he hands the Fender to me, taking Ruby for himself.

It's entirely appropriate that I'm left playing electric lead, because I'm the only one with any real guitar chops. But it's Telly's guitar, and I shudder and breathe deep.

Kyle is setting up drums in the form of a cardboard box, the metal edge of my desk, a lampshade, a set of bongos, and a half-full coin jar.

We tune up, all shaggy.

Javon cranks the bass. The house shudders, and a hanging photo of Grandpa crashes to the floor.

Thank god Mimi's out tonight.

"In Bloom" is an old Nirvana tune. The chords are mostly half barres, which you want to shred, then play hiccupy. I show Nick and Ryan how to do this, but they're pretty hopeless. That's okay, because on acoustic nobody's gonna hear 'em anyway.

"Man," I say, "let's do it."

We suck ourselves quiet. It's been a long time since we've made noise together. Till now, Telly's always been the frontman.

I tap my foot. "One, two . . .

". . . one-Two-THREE-*FO'!*"

We crash open in a monstrous frenzy of power chords and frantic drumming. Kyle is everywhere, jumping up and down with his drumsticks, then he thrusts out his chest and screams. Raw and ragged. Even though he's not miked we can hear him over the amplifiers. Javon plugs the holes with an unrelated bass line. I have no idea where he's coming from, but by being out of sync, maybe he's finding a new sync.

Normally, "In Bloom" takes about four minutes to play, but four minutes into the song we are barely warmed up. Not even sweating. Nick bends over and pops my cable into the distortion box. I try a lead. Make it sound like a drunk bumblebee. Then I buckle that bumblebee into a roller coaster.

Whoa!

I crank the volume.

We do song after song—Chili Peppers, White Stripes, Crossfade, Queens of the Stone Age—and everything sounds the same—fuzzy, sloppy, incoherent.

But incoherence can be a form of coherence.

Just as unhinged volume can be a form of silence.

Just as jagged edge can be a form of butterfly.

That is the lesson of art, whether music or poetry.

Opposites blur and become one. If you open your mind, that is.

After a while, everybody's pink and sweaty. Kyle grabs a T-shirt off the floor, wipes his face. The house feels fragile, like maybe we've cracked some beams, tilted the floor a degree or two.

Nick says, "Hey, man, do sumpin' solo."

They look at me, wiped and smiley. "Yeah, yeah, just you."

I hand the Fender to Nick, who hands me Ruby.

I sit on the bed. As I ponder what to play, I noodle on my Telly tune, my own little bit of Beethoven, which starts high on the tenth and twelfth frets and hops like a bunny down the neck and which is held together with an E–F#–G bass stitch.

Jordan says, "Yeah, yeah, play that."

So I do. I play my Telly piece. No lyrics. Maybe someday, not yet.

It's just a few motifs and configurations that remind me of him, sewn together. Among them are the transition from D to E minor, and from C to A minor, and the haunting quality of F#7, especially when you hammer the middle finger.

"Tune to Telly" starts a train, and I jump on board. In my mind, we're eight again, rushing down the trail to Longfellow Creek, Grandpa limping and cussing behind us. Then we're in our toddle days, flying the zip swing at Lincoln Park.

Days of aching perfection.

Glimmering immortality.

Because the tune is still under construction, I stitch in a bit of "Here Comes the S-O-N." I still can't play the run-up or rundown, but I can play the intro, which is a nice mix of chording and picking. At first, I play these clean. No bend, fuzz, or hammer, because that's how Telly played it, unshowy, like a saint. Then I slow it down, deepen it, bend a note. Hear an echo. Circle back. Hear the echo louder this time, a golden truth. Just what that truth is, I can't say. But I could do a thousand drafts of a poem and still not get as close to the truth as that one bent note.

When I glance up, I see their eyes shining. Tears are running down Jordan's cheeks.

Something's happened to me, too. I've just played better than ever, and all I did was play from my gut.

Whoa!

It's too much.

So I plant a fuzzy E. Pick up the pace. Crunch it. Sugar it with pinkie M&M's.

It's time we stopped being so sad and started talkin' the blues.

I sing:

"Just sittin' here strummin' Ruby,
Got taurine on my mind.
Just sittin' here strummin' Ruby,
Got taurine on my mind.
Gotta getta good night's sleep.
Or soon I will go blind."

"Oh," Ryan says, "I got one."

He leaps up, puffs out his chest, sings:

"Just lyin' on a beach down in Texas,
Time is half past three.
Down in Texas, lyin' on a sandy beach,
Time is half past three.
Gotta bare-naked lady in my arms,
Name of Angelina Jolie."

"Hey, my turn," Kyle says.

And he basically repeats Ryan's beach rhyme, except he ends it this way:

"Gotta bare-naked lady in my arms,
Name of Sweet Mimi."

Quickly, everything descends and discombobulates into blues chaos, with everybody pitching in. On the spot, we compose a song of collective genius, all about eating grapes, flunking out, jacking off, and sleeping with moms.

We call the song "Walkin', Talkin' West Seattle Four-Hour Hard-On Blues."

We call our band, for tonight anyway, "Erectile Dysfunction."

Between verses, Nick hands me a sleeping pill and glass of water. Later, I take another pill. And still later, a third.

By now, though, it's late—mystical trough late. I'm seeing halos around everything. My thicks are thinning out. One by one, they disappear.

Nick and Kyle are the only ones left. Nick slips Ruby out of my hands.

I weave into the bathroom, piss. The toilet handle is too far away.

Nick flushes for me, and he and Kyle walk me into Telly's room. Sit me on Telly's bed. Nick pulls off my shoes. Kyle stands there, staring at me.

"Dude," he says, "your time has come."

Nick goes out of the room and comes back with the dildo-shaped Christmas candle. He lights the candle and puts it on the bedside table. They tug off my jeans, roll me into Telly's bed.

Tuck me in.

"Think I'll take off now," Kyle says. "Sleep, dude. Tomorrow— today—will be history."

Now it's just Nick and me. Everything is all jagged and fuzzy. Nick has dragged in Ruby's rocking chair. He curls up in it, blanket over his shoulders.

But he gets up one last time. Takes a picture off the dresser. A picture of Telly and me. Taken at the Puyallup Fair three years ago. We're wearing matching straw cowboy hats. Telly's holding a deck of trick cards.

Nick puts the picture on the bedside table, moves the candle so Telly's and my faces glow.

Then he goes to the closet. Slides open the door, reaches up, and lifts down the black box that holds all that's left on this earth of my brother. Telly the physical being, that is. Just a few spoonfuls of gray, gritty dust.

He places the box on the table beside the picture. Beside the candle.

Then he wraps himself again in the blanket. Curls up in the rocking chair. Folds his arms around Ruby.

Flickers out.

chapter 33

The window in Telly's room is wide open. Bird chatter breezes in. But also clanking wrench sounds. Banging the bars of the scaffolding.

I'm trying to wake up, but my heart isn't beating.

Molecule by molecule, twitching knuckle by twitching knuckle, I come to life. Feel a pimple form on the flat line of my brain.

I inch out of bed. Poke my raw face out the window.

The scaffolding has been set up on the north side of the house. Nick is on the high platform swiping purple paint. Javon stands on the ground, trimming a basement window. His Zoom LeBron VIs stand primly on the back stoop, safe from dripping paint.

Jordan is banging and cussing the scaffolding.

I step into the shower, crank it hot. Soap up, shampoo.

Standing there, all sudsy, I remember the day.

Fuck!

I have no idea what time it is.

I open the shower door and jog, foamy and drippy, to my bedroom. It's 3:11 p.m.

Graduation is at five.

I've slept something like twelve hours.

Thanks to the Celtic poetess and Angelina Jolie, compressed into whispering pills, I have slept my first real night's sleep in months.

A dreamless, dungeonless, dragonless sleep.

All night long these two beauties have patched holes in my brain. One night's work can't patch all the holes, but they have patched some of the big ones.

I jump back into the shower. Shave my seen-only-from-a-certain-angle-in-certain-light mustache. Rinse off. Towel dry.

Rub Old Spice Red Zone—"The Official Scent of Confidence"—on my pits.

My phone is *bbbrrrackk*ing.

Kyle.

"Get your ass movin', dude!"

Mimi barges into my room wearing a short-at-both-ends cocktail dress. You can see the freckles on her boobs. It's not really appropriate for graduation, but then I'm not graduating.

"Oh. My. Gawwwdddd!" She surveys the wreckage of last night. Pivots. "ZIP ME UP!"

I zip her up.

"Wear this!" She yanks out my charcoal suit and a white dress shirt. "And brush your dang hair. It looks like a wet mop."

I brush my dang hair, put on my charcoal pants and dark shoes. But no way am I wearing a white dress shirt. No way am I wearing that suit jacket.

I snap open Murchison. Gaze upon the folded black Navy uniform. Last worn by David O. H. Cosgrove II. Probably in the waning days of World War II, after he saw the shimmer and broke through.

I lift out the jacket. Unfold it. Flap it loose. Dust it off. Put my nose to the mothball-soaked fibers. Two gold stripes on each sleeve. Double-breasted. Brass buttons.

I go into Telly's room, open his closet, riffle through his yellow T-shirts, choose a Tony Hawk, strawberry trim.

Classic Telly.

I put on the yellow T-shirt, then slide into David Cosgrove's Navy jacket.

I check myself in the mirror. The jacket fits, basically. A little loose maybe. The yellow T-shirt and gold stripes kind of match.

As for style, who the hell knows.

My eyes lock onto the black box on Telly's bedside table. I open the box and slip the plastic bag that holds the last of Telly into my jacket pocket.

chapter 34

Taft High School has one of the best jazz bands in the city. Led by Clarence P. Tillmann Jr.

Mr. Tillmann played with Duke Ellington, Count Basie, and Dizzy Gillespie back in the golden days. Played trumpet for Billie Holiday in the Seattle jazz clubs, in the smoky-blue days before World War II. Roomed with Ray Charles on Jackson Street. Played in the famous Frank Sinatra band, Quincy Jones conductor. Played echo trumpet to Miles Davis's solo on "Bitches Brew."

Mr. Tillmann is the only person at Taft who outranks Gupti. Not in title, but in reputation. He's a shriveled prune of a man. Wears a signature bolo tie that says "Count." Whether that means "Count time," "Count Basie," or "Count Dracula," nobody knows.

When Mimi and I get to the Kenny G, Mr. Tillmann is rehearsing "Pick Up the Pieces" with the jazz band. Waving his wand. Grooving his shoulders. He catches my eye as I come down the aisle.

It's 4:27 p.m.

"Good luck, baby," Mimi says, and kisses my cheek.

She shudders again at the sight of my Navy jacket, then wanders off to find a seat. I climb the stage stairs. Kyle pulls me into the wings.

"Dude," he says, fingering my gold stripes. "*Whoa! History—history!*"

Above us, Kong looks stoic and bewildered. It's sad to think what we put animals through. The indignities we thrust on them. As Kyle babbles about technical details, I transmit a little message to Kong telepathically:

"I'm sorry, man."

I'm starting to shake. Not just my hands, but my whole core. All the weeks and months pondering today, not quite believing it would happen. Now it's here. People are walking into the Kenny G. Student ushers are passing out programs. My name is in those programs. Soon everyone will be staring at me.

And where will I be?

Standing in the cupped hand of the Velcro Kong.

Playing a cherry red guitar.

I watch the people filter into the auditorium. Frank Conway wanders in. He's wearing a dark necktie. A green leather jacket. His guitar philosophy echoes in my head:

Learn the rules . . . then break them.

Don't take shortcuts.

Practice a thousand times.

Frank shambles up the aisle, looking for a seat. Spots Mimi. Hesitates. Turns down the row, speaks to her. She looks surprised. Flashes all her lights. He sits beside her.

Good. Good.

"Dude," Kyle says, waving for me to follow.

Nick and a couple of sound techs have the mikes ready. Mr. Takakawa is there, too. He's classically trained. Doesn't usually deal with guys like me, who can't read music.

The sound techs show me how to wear the wireless headset. The mike is dinky—no bigger than a golf tee. The Ric, too, will be wireless. But unlike me, Ricky will be wearing a safety harness.

"This is a very unusual setup," Mr. Takakawa says, surveying the Velcro Kong. "Do you know what you're doing?"

"Absolutely," Kyle says, nodding vigorously.

He wraps an arm over me, pulls me away. "Dude," he says, "Javon and I have made some minor alterations to the program. We're gonna pipe you through Fat Phyllis and Big Bertha."

Whoa! These are the Ford- and Toyota-pickup-size amps used at Taft football games. Together they can carry a whisper to the ears of thousands.

Or enough volume to loosen the bolts on the walls of the Kenny G.

Fat Phyllis and Big Bertha have been rolled into the wings. One on each side of the stage.

I shake my head. "Way too much volume. Just use the regular sound system."

"No worries," Kyle says. "Javon can modify and modulate. We're going for a slightly rawer sound, you see."

"But it's not a raw song."

"True," Kyle says, "but the dude playing it *is* raw." He slaps my back. "Just don't hit any sour notes."

When I glance out again, the front half of the auditorium is jammed. People are climbing the stairs and flooding the balconies. It's beginning to feel like the USS *Gabriel Trask*. Bow going up, stern going down. Ready to plunge to the bottom.

Then I see Katie. Gary Death is with her, pushing Agnes in her wheelchair. They roll up the aisle. Katie is wearing her tickle-the-ass Beyoncé wig and a little skirt. Guys are cutting eyes.

An usher guides them to a wheelchair parking space about two thirds back. Katie gestures toward the front of the Kenny G. The usher shakes his head.

I go down the stairs and up the aisle. Katie says, "She can't hear anything from way back here."

I tap the two gold stripes on my sleeve. "I'll take care of this."

The usher backs off.

I'm a bit awed, because here's Katie looking healthy and normal, and I know it's not true. Twice in four weeks, she's been hooked to tubes.

That's the way it is, though. It comes and goes. Good days and bad. Today must be a good day.

Gary Death smiles, shakes my hand. "Good luck, lieutenant."

Agnes beams. "Float a turd."

"I plan to," I say.

I expand my shoulders, for authority, and we roll up the aisle. The Navy jacket helps me look official, but the yellow T-shirt might throw folks.

I push Agnes up the ramp onto the stage. Park her in the wings. It's gotta be one of the best views in the house. Fetch folding chairs for Katie and Gary.

"You sure this is okay?" Katie asks.

"It's okay with me," I say.

Then I'm gone.

Slipping backstage and out the door into the corridor. Needing to sit down. Breathe. Maybe throw up.

Or maybe just bang out the exit and keep on going. Cross the baseball field, hop a bus, and be gone, all the way to some foreign country. Like Greece, with its whitewashed houses above the blue sea. Or the Sierras, and live in the woods, in a hollow tree.

But instead I go into the music room, which Mr. Takakawa has left unlocked for the moment, and then into the storage room, where all the instruments are kept. A forest of hanging trombones. Vast mesas of kettledrums. A regiment of violins and violas in stenciled black cases. Hooded double basses.

I sit on the edge of an old metal desk. In the dim light, I make out key-carved names and dates going back to the 1960s.

My whole being is shaking and quaking.

Somewhere inside me, a nuclear reactor is coming unhinged. Meltdown feels inevitable.

I stare at my hands. Observe them scientifically, as someone else's hands, not mine.

How'm I gonna form a chord? Pick a note?

The clink of a hammer begins to fall against the anvil of my brain.

I crave taurine.

I crave NoDoz.

Bayer, Tylenol, Aleve—anything to depressurize the internal reactor that is about to explode.

Then the door to the music room opens.

Somebody walks in.

It's gotta be Kyle, Nick, or one of my other thicks. Or possibly Mr. Takakawa. But when I lean over and peer out, I see Clarence P. Tillmann Jr.

Even though I'm sitting in the dim light of the instrument storage room, half hidden by a tuba case, in the shadow of a cello, he seems to know exactly where I am.

He ducks under a hanging bassoon.

"Hello, Jonathan."

So the shriveled jazz god knows my name.

"Hey."

He sits beside me on the edge of the desk. He's a lot shorter than me. But his hands are big trumpet-player hands. Knuckly and gnarled.

Time and jazz have carved deep lines in his face.

"Confidence," Mr. Tillmann says, "is overrated. All the great ones started out scared. Scared is the country we live in, Jonathan. Scared gets you one mile farther down the road. Gets you to the top of the tree. You do your best work when you're scared. Play your best notes."

"Yeah," I say, "but I'm not great."

He shakes his head. "Even the great ones put on their shoes one at a time. How do you put on your shoes?"

"One at a time," I say.

"And they reach for the toilet tissues just like everybody else." He laughs, wheezily. "There are two kinds of musicians, Jonathan: those who know how to play, and those who know how to play when the curtain goes up." He taps my head. "This is your real instrument. Use it to shrink the Kenny G to the size of your kitchen. Then imagine your best friends sitting around the table. And play for them, just them. Or if there's one special person out there, conjure 'im up. Sinatra never sang to more than one person, and it was usually a woman in a silk nightie.

And Miles never played to more than a couple of lone souls standing on a midnight bridge. Your mind can take you wherever you want to go, Jonathan. Just conjure."

"Hey," I say. "I'm pretty good at that."

"I know you are," Mr. Tillmann says. He gazes at the instruments stacked, hanging, forever waiting—and inhales the room.

"I like it in here, too," he says.

He checks his watch.

"Let's go tune that guitar."

• • •

When Mr. Tillmann and I emerge into the backstage area, Kyle is pacing like a caged cougar. He spots me, and his whole body says *Whew!*

"We thought, dude—" Kyle says.

"No, we didn't," Nick says.

Nick snaps open the silver guitar case, hands me the Ric. I strap Ricky on my shoulder. For all his sleek lines and contours, he's heavy. Unlike my fairy-light Ruby.

"So," Mr. Tillmann says, "this is the guitar everybody's talkin' about."

"Yeah," Kyle says. "This is a Rickenbacker three-sixty six. Sonically, the coolest guitar of all time."

Mr. Tillmann shakes his head. "Too bad. It's going straight into a display case after this concert—you know, that big glass case outside Dr. Jacobson's office. This'll likely be the first and last time it ever gets played in a proper concert."

"*Whoa!*" Kyle says.

Nick says, "That's tragic."

Mr. Tillmann nods. "By order of the principal herself. That guitar is just too famous for its own good."

Kyle pokes me. "All the more reason to crank it, dude."

Great! Now I've got Ricky on my conscience. Can't let him down, either.

Everybody—even a guitar—wants a bite out of my ass.

Mr. Tillmann reaches inside his jacket and pulls out a little mouth tuner.

"What time did the king eat breakfast?"

"Early," I say.

"You got it," Mr. Tillmann says.

We tune the Ric.

E . . . A . . . D . . . G . . . B . . . E—Elvis Ate a Damn Good Breakfast Early.

Pipe the sound out of Fat Phyllis's little toe at about one-thousandth of a decibel.

"Mmm," Mr. Tillmann says. "That dog'll hunt."

He notices the little brass plate screwed on the side of the Ric. Puts on his reading glasses. Bends down.

"For Tel—"

"Te-*lem*-a-chus," I say.

He reads Eddie Vedder's engraved message: "RIP and keep in touch."

"If I remember my Homer," he says, "Telemachus was the son of Odysseus, that brave fellow who fought the Trojans and the Cyclops and hanky-pankied around with witches and nymphs."

"Yeah," I say. "You remember."

Nick hands me a capo. I clamp on the second fret.

"Your parents must be literary types," Mr. Tillmann says.

"Extremely not," I say.

Nick says, "His real name was Edward."

Kyle says, "Teddy."

"So how did he come to be called Telemachus?" Mr. Tillmann asks.

Kyle and Nick point at me.

"In my day," Mr. Tillmann says, "we gave each other all sorts of names—T-Bone, Duke, Muddy, Dizzy—but never a name as complex as Telemachus."

"He was pretty complex," Kyle says.

"Yeah, but he was basic, too," Nick says.

"Uh-huh," Mr. Tillmann says. "But that doesn't answer my question. Why Telemachus?"

"Yeah, dude," Kyle says. "I never fully, cognitively understood that either. Explain it to all of us."

"It's a little abstract," I say. "Remember Miss Scardino's class, when we read *The Odyssey*?"

"Yeah."

"Well, Telly and me were talking, and he asked, who would you rather be, Odysseus, the man of action, fighting for glory, getting blown all over the place by Poseidon, living by your wits, never resting, never anything in the middle, always on the edge? Or Telemachus, who stayed behind, took long walks on the beach, probably put his ear to a few seashells, wrote poetry, and messed around on his lute?"

"And he chose Telemachus?" Mr. Tillmann asks.

"No," I say. "He chose Odysseus. I chose Telemachus."

"Then why call *him*—?"

"That's how we worked," I say. "To bring out the other side in each other. I'd bring out Telemachus in him, and he'd bring out Odysseus in me. Just like I brought out the guitar player in him, and he brought out the poet in me."

"Hey, Jonathan," Nick says. "That poem . . . you know, that big one you're always messin' on . . ."

" 'Tales of Telemachus'?"

"Yeah, that one. Is that about him or you?"

"Correct," I say.

Mr. Tillmann reaches out, straightens my guitar strap. "Question is," he says, "which one of you is gonna play that guitar?"

"*Whoa!*" Kyle says. "You just watch."

chapter 35

It's a few minutes past five o'clock.

Gupti's sitting on stage in her black academic gown, saffron sash. Forcing smiles all over the place. I can tell she's antsy to get started.

Birdwell's there, too, in *his* black gown, purple sash, with other senior representatives of the faculty. They sit two rows deep behind the podium.

The Kenny G is full, right up to the balconies. Out in the crowd, a few seats to the right of Mimi, a few rows farther back, is Vic, the father I do not know. A baby clings to his neck. He's sitting beside an Asian woman barely half his size.

Right away, I know it's their baby. It's in the squirmy, presleep stage. Kind of mini-monkeying all over him. Vic cozies it under his chin. Pats its rump.

That's sure not the way he patted my rump.

Or Telly's.

But maybe—*maybe!*—he's not the same anymore. God knows, every pat on that little ass might be another step down Vic's evolutionary road.

The fact is, he's here. He's not tightening lug nuts.

In back, at the entrance to the Kenny G, there's a ripple. People crane. A few even stand to get a better look.

Eddie—The Vedder—strides up the aisle. Brooding rock star. Skater poet.

He's wearing a flannel shirt, black leather vest. Glasses. Average as anybody, yet lit differently. Hair pulled back into a ponytail, and he's got a scraggly beard. He trolls for a seat. He could sit in the VIP section—my invitation included a pass—but instead he bounds upstairs into the balcony and squeezes between two unsuspecting grandmothers, who don't catch on.

It's a nice move. Humility. Anonymity.

Jeezus! Everybody showed up.

The lights go down. Go up on the jazz band.

Mr. Tillmann steps to the mike. "Here's a little chart the senior jazz ensemble wrote called 'Wildcat Symphony.' Gonna play it in the Count Basie style, key of life."

He lifts his wand. The jazz band crashes into the tune. Mr. Tillmann shimmies, swings his shoulders. A clarinet player bursts out of her chair, blows a wild stream of notes. Behind her, three trombone players leap up, blast away.

I'm standing in the wings, running my fingers through the note formations of "Crossing the River Styx."

Of all guitars I've ever played, the Ric has the tightest, smoothest action. The strings are so finely aligned on the neck that the slightest pressure gives you contact and sound. Most guitar strings cut into your fingers, but the Ric's are as soft and pliable as egg yolks.

They are the same strings that Telly once touched.

Mr. Ridenaur, the head counselor, is making a speech about socks. He wants to give every graduating senior a used sock donated by the faculty. He points to a large cardboard box on the edge of the stage. Asks every senior to take one sock after picking up a diploma.

"So, seniors, abide by this strategy, for it will serve you well in life: before you speak that first idiotic thought, stuff a sock in your mouth."

"*Psst*—Jonathan!"

Uh-oh, Birdwell.

"Don't you know how to spell?"

He flutters up in his academic gown. I turn the neck of the Ric to fend him off.

"I've counted more than one hundred typos in your Cosgrove memoir, Jonathan. What about spell checker? What about grammar checker?"

He doesn't even mention that I turned in the book on time—*on time!*

"I read the whole thing last night, Jonathan," he says. "All one hundred and eighty-four pages. Did you even look at the words as you typed? Let me tell you, let me tell you—"

"Hold up!" I say. "Don't tell me! DO NOT TELL ME!"

Birdwell's eyes bulge. "Ah," he says, "of course. Now's not the time or place."

He points to Gupti. "She knows exactly how I feel."

Gupti is standing. In three long strides she's at the podium. Her braided ponytail is visible only where it intersects with her saffron sash.

She lets the light settle on her tall frame. Beams professionally, a full sweep of the auditorium. "Graduating seniors, parents, faculty, and staff . . ."

Kyle nudges me. "Dude, remember, Kong has a bad foot, so stay centered. Now, go on out there and write some history."

Nick leans close. "Go for it, man."

I'm feeling strangely detached from them. Butterflies, yes.

But also numb. Mummified. As if I'm wrapped in some spiritual gauze.

Everything in my life seems to be the material from which this gauze is made: the death of Telly, my thirst for taurine, months of sleep deprivation, my performance anxieties, David Cosgrove—his death and life.

Plus the fact that here, in the audience, are all of the movers and shakers in my life.

Thicks, thins, teachers.

Mimi.

Biological Vic.

Beak-nosed Birdwell.

Shambly, coffee-addicted Frank Conway.

Katie, hiding her illness under a wig.

Agnes, who wants to be an angel.

Gary Death.

Even The Vedder is here. Emerging from his fame cocoon to flit among the ordinary moths.

Normally I'd have the jitters playing to The Vedder alone. Thor-voiced singer, crunching guitar player that he is. Now I'm playing to him and twelve hundred others.

At such a time, all the safety of thickness can't prop you up.

You're on your own.

Standing on the guardrail of the bridge.

Where you gotta either fall or fly.

It's like they're out there, David and Telly, but not in the audience. Maybe in the foyer, sipping bottled water. Jabbering with each other.

Standing on the guardrail of the bridge, you see this.

Both your aloneness and connectedness.

It's not about stuffing socks in your mouth. It's about pulling them out.

Hacking up the snot.

Spitting it out.

And shouting, "Life!"

If Telly were here, in my place, he would rise like the sun. Shake his golden head. His fingers would fly up and down the Ric, striking sparks. He would be great.

Me, I'm not great.

I'm just gonna play how I feel.

And leave it at that.

Gupti's rambling.

". . . one of our finest young poets and the youngest winner *ever* of the Quatch, the most prestigious student poetry competition in our state. And now a gifted biographer. Yesterday, he presented Dr. Bramwell with his latest achievement."

She holds up the manuscript that contains all of my taurine-fueled words about David Cosgrove. Waves it high above her head.

"These pages tell the story of a man—old, blind, and forgotten.

"Yet an Everyman. A timeless truth seeker, as all of us must be, in every phase of our lives.

"Jonathan has titled this memoir *Swimming Toward the Shimmer*. This morning, I began reading—and my oh my . . ."

A sweet sigh.

That fades to a frown.

"I do not approve of every word or phrase. Lord knows, some of this"—Gupti smacks the manuscript—"is undercooked. But then I think of the proverb 'The tiger grows strong supping on raw meat.'

"We learn from these pages . . ."

Gupti talks on and on.

She talks about hearing me sing and play guitar. That rainy winter day Kyle and I broke into the music room. Cracked open the Ric.

She talks about Telly.

"He wasn't just a brother, he was a *twin* brother."

Everybody knows this already. But it's always nice to be martyred once again. To let them see the arrows sticking out of your ass.

"How should one deal with grief?" Gupti asks. "Well, I can think of no better way than to transform it into art—the art of the heart. Poetry. History. Music. Jonathan, you are an artist!"

She smiles into the microphone.

"I've asked Jonathan to perform my all-time favorite song. None of us has heard him in rehearsal. This is strictly a student-owned production. He'll be playing a beautiful guitar donated by Mr. Eddie Vedder, in memory of Jonathan's brother. So without further ado"—she waves my manuscript above her head again—"I give you Jonathan!"

• • •

Darkness falls on the Kenny G.

A tavern light goes up on the jazz band.

Mr. Tillmann lifts his wand. Whispers "a-one-an-a-two . . ." The band bursts into "Pick Up the Pieces."

Overhead, the ceiling begins thunking and clunking. Javon,

up in his techno bird nest, toggles a stick that plants the hook onto the loop behind the Velcro Kong. Javon entices Kong from the wings, lures him front and center. Fringes him in midnight jungle green. Suddenly, he's not a prop. He's a beast. Primal. Staring across the void.

The audience gasps. Feels Kong's power. Cameras flash.

Kyle nudges me. "Crack it, dude!"

I step onto the pallet. Jordan cranks the lever. Halfway up, Javon fires a pin light at me.

Whoa!

I'm shining like a polished spoon.

The light is impossibly bright—the Star of Bethlehem, both near and far.

Up close, I can see the staples and duct tape on Kong. All the amateur workmanship. The water stains. Yet he seems noble and alive. Facing the horde. Ready to die for his honor.

It's just a short hop through the air into his cupped hand.

I grip the Ric. Make the leap.

Feel tension on Ricky's safety harness as we fly through the air.

Javon tracks me.

The Ric and I land in Kong's hand.

Kong wobbles. Back and forth . . .

Centers himself.

Javon's pin is achingly bright. But nothing is brighter than the Ric.

It has to be the cherry-reddest guitar in the world.

Not a scratch or chafe or nick. It looks unreal.

I reach into my pocket. Open the Ziploc bag.

Grab the last handful of my brother.

Hold up my fist. Let his dust fall. Sprinkling the air.

Javon's light catches it.

Telly falls in quicksilver particles.

Dusting my shoes, the palm of Kong, and the Ric.

But Telly's dust doesn't let go that easily.

The very last of him clings to me, a faint resin on my pickin' and chordin' fingers.

I adjust my headset. Reach into my pocket for a pick—I have at least twenty, just in case.

Choose the thickest of all.

Position my left hand on Ricky's neck.

Speak into the impossibly bright shimmer. Light so bright everything else is dark.

Into twelve hundred sets of ears that may or may not be there.

Because in my mind, I'm stepping into the kitchen.

Sitting down at the table.

Just me and my thicks.

My voice shakes.

"Here's a little Pinky Toe for you. Sorry if I'm pitchy. Listen at your own risk."

chapter 36

The intro to "Crossing the River Styx" is a series of fast notes, with one short frill and one long one. It's a ditty I've messed up countless times in practice because I'm not much of a picker.

But now I don't mess up. I play it metronome perfect.

Each note a thunderous sound blasting out of Big Bertha and Fat Phyllis and soaking into the state-of-the-art acoustic walls of the Kenny G.

Raw power.

Yet innocent, as Gupti would want it.

The taste of cotton candy.

I sense the Ric knows the song better than I do. Because when I reach the end of the intro and am supposed to start singing, I don't. I feel a great desire to go back and play the intro again.

Play it my way.

And I do. This time, though, I don't sound metronome perfect.

Or frilly. Or sweet.

I open my eyes on the dark bright glare of the auditorium.

I can't see a thing. But then through a hole in the glare I see Vic and that little baby clinging to his neck. Guess that baby is my half brother or sister. Or something like that.

I slow down "Crossing the River Styx."

The Ric wants me to bend a few notes, so I do. I play a bending lick, off B, way up on the tenth fret. Push it up a whole step—which is hard enough off the B string, but the Ric wants me to push it *two* whole steps—a gigantic leap. An aching arch.

The notes that bleed out are the bluest blue I've ever played. Yet lullaby, too.

The Ric seems to know all about it. The Ric seems to know everything. About me, Telly—even this baby.

I fire off another round of notes. They are totally unfamiliar. But they sound tight. They ring perfectly.

Jeezus!

How did I do that?

This is no time or place to be experimenting or improvising, but that's exactly what I've just done—and it worked.

When I open my mouth to sing, my voice comes out greasy. Not as pink lemonade, the way the Pinky Toe singer does it. But as a midnight cheeseburger, slopped with onions and ketchup:

I'm crossing the River Styx.
From Charon I wrest the oar,
To speed my soul to the Plutonian Shore.

These lyrics have always tasted like some kind of sugary Greek goo, but now I'm starved for them.

'Cause I've got to be free,
To lie upone the breast of Persephone
In the land of Nevermore.

When I sing "'Cause I've got to be free," I give it everything. Bend it far. Feel it deep where the loneliest butterfly flutters.

Because I do have to be free.

Free of Gupti and everybody else who wants something out of me.

I add another blues run—the tightest yet.

A raw wail in the night.

Holy shit!

Clearly the Ric does not mind my ignorance.

I open the kitchen door and step outside. Go to the edge of the cliff.

When a baby eagle leaps from its nest for the first time, how high can it fly? That's my dilemma. Because now I want to go all the way up to the sun.

When I open my eyes again, I see, through the glare, an old man. Gray beard. Walt Whitmanesque. Sitting there.

I focus on him.

Rip through a run of hard notes—all rocketing from the basic "Crossing the River Styx" theme, but firing in different directions, then interlacing in the sky.

Fountains of sound.

Intricacies beyond all of my powers as a guitar player, even on the best day of my life.

I don't dare think about this. All I know is, I could fall out of the sky any second.

But it's nice to soar. Up close to the sun.

Deep inside one of these riffs, I hear a voice. A kind of echo.

Javon must be messing with me. Adding some kind of talk-box effect.

I play the riff again. Hear the voice again—*damn!*

Now everything I'm doing on the Ric is new and untried.

Flying higher and higher. Shuddering up my spine and down to my tailbone.

But also shuddering up and down Kong's spine. Because we are moving together. In a jungle dance.

"Crossing the River Styx" is really two songs. The first half is a distinct melody, to be played with exactitude, which I have done more successfully than I could've dreamed.

Stitched it both even and jagged.

Played it straight. Bent it blue.

The second half is operatic. Open to interpretation.

It's the easiest part. Just the chords C–F, G–F. Repeated. Maybe toss in a minor or a ninth. And the chanting:

Crossing the River Styx,
To the land of Nevermore.

I swap to a crunching strum. Crunch is a muscle approach to guitar, and in all my practices, I've never used it.

But now I do. Each down stroke sends a jackhammer-like shiver through Kong.

I'm staring into the blinding light. Hearing the ghostly talk-box echo.

Who the hell . . . ?

And then I know.

I peer through the glare. At the back of the Kenny G, I see a lone guy in a yellow T-shirt. Slumped in his chair. Watching me.

As Kong sways back and forth, I focus on him.

Begin to chant lines from my masterpiece, "Tales of Telemachus." Just a little chaos.

"Where do we go in the night, o brother?"

I hear the echo: *"Where do we go?"*

"When will the rain fall?"

I hear the echo: *"When will the rain fall?"*
Kong weaves back and forth. Throbs primally.

"Who knows?"
"Who knows?"

His voice is so alive. So part of me.
I crush the strings.
Scream: *"ME LEAST OF ALL!"*
This time, though, I hear no echo. It's like he's disagreeing.
Just like always.
Protesting my self-doubt.
Because Telly builds me up.
Believes in me.
Even now.
Even as Kong leans forward, ready to dive for a vine.
I press my back into his chest. Throw all my weight to get him centered again.
But it's not gonna happen.
I scurry through a reflection of "Crossing the River Styx."
Play with all the adrenaline and taurine left inside me. Bend the notes till the walls of the Kenny G suck inward.
A gigantic decibel flourish.
A final stitch.

Ain't it a bitch.

We're going down.

Kong drops away.

Falls face first onto the stage.

Amid a bedlam of leaping faculty members, flapping gowns.

Ricky and I swing across the stage, in a swooping arc, me clinging to his neck.

I'm thinking about how damn valuable this guitar is.

Probably the most valuable instrument in the whole United States system of public education.

Worth a fortune on eBay.

The strain of my weight is gonna break the harness. Send Ricky crashing to the floor. This is gonna happen any second.

So I let go.

And fall.

I fall, fall, fall into Javon's blinding light.

Swim toward the shimmer.

Thinking of my brother.

Thinking of Telemachus.

chapter 37

Craacckk!

Something happens in my bones when I hit the stage.

But I'm so focused on the Ric that I feel no pain.

I rise up on an elbow and track the transit of Ricky as he swoops above the stage.

Watch how, with all of my unloosened weight, the momentum flings him into the wall of the proscenium arch, smashing him against it.

Watch how he jerks like a hooked fish.

Watch him erupt—in a burst of short-circuitry, a geyser of notes, blasting from some computerized memory cell that mashes all of my previous "Crossing the River Styx" sounds into something even more frenzied and agonized.

Hear the notes screaming through every sweating pore of Big Bertha and Fat Phyllis.

Till a flame leaps out of the F holes. Flares up. Engulfs Ricky.

The Kenny G—the whole school community—gasps.

Katie drops beside me.

Agnes rolls up.

We are all—everyone, from Gupti on down to the last usher—staring transfixedly at Ricky.

The flaming guitar. The tortured prince.

Dangling. Swaying.

We watch the flames die down. The smoke clear. See the beautiful cherry body streaked black.

A hush falls over the Kenny G.

A single, twangy note pops out of Ricky.

Then a burst of notes. And another.

Then spasms of them.

Remembered from way back when Telly played "Here Comes the Son."

Burned and dying, Ricky remembers.

The contrapuntal stuff.

The bass run.

The uplick.

The downlick.

All the angel notes.

Dewdrops of sunlight.

Premonitions of death.

Ricky plays them all.

Nails it.

Nails it fast and hard and forever.

Ends on a final sublime D.

Ching!

chapter 38

In that paralyzing pause, when god tries to explain to twelve hundred people what just happened, Agnes is the first to act.

She reaches down from her wheelchair and grabs my headset. Puts the golf-tee-size mike to her lips.

Lifts her voice to the audience:

"Free the swimmers in the dark," she says.

Fat Phyllis and Big Bertha carry these words to every last eardrum.

"Free the swimmers in the dark," Agnes repeats.

Then she says, "Never give up. Never give up!"

Pain is shooting through my right leg. Throbbing in my ankle. Nick is there, helping me up.

Kyle steps beside Agnes, takes up the chant.

"Never give up!" he shouts.

He waves for the crowd to follow.

And they do.

It starts out slowly. But it builds. And it keeps building till it becomes a tidal roar.

"NEVER GIVE UP!"

People are standing.

Then the whole *fucking* house goes crazy.

chapter 39

I go into the hospital with a broken leg and broken ankle.

Specifically, a compound fracture of the tibia. Plus an acute hairline break in the talus.

Plus a host of contusions and lacerations.

They operate. Put in titanium screws and a metal plate.

I now have a bionic ankle.

The nurses jack me with painkillers in the form of a sweet, intoxicating intravenous drip.

A wondrous syrup.

My own log cabin in the woods.

Drowsiness falls drop by drop upon my brain.

And I sleep.

A dragonless, dungeonless sleep.

Day and night, the sleep of the weary mind. The comatose soul.

And in those rare minutes when I'm not sleeping—but spooning some bletchy hospital gruel or watching some blond weather lady on TV—I'm thinking about a nap.

Visitors come and go, but they all blur.

A couple days later, Mimi checks me out of the hospital. Rolls me outside in a wheelchair, into the thin Seattle sun. My right leg is elevated in a thigh-high cast. I'm holding a helium balloon that says "Get Well Soon."

I, too, feel a lightness. In parts of me that have long felt leaden.

My body is achy. Scratchy, squirmy, throbby. But the ether that I breathe—my own mix of air, for we all breathe our own unique blend—is somehow purer. I take it in. Breathe deeply.

Don't pretend to understand.

Kyle and Nick are leaning against the Volks in the drop-off lane.

Mimi kisses me and races off on a round of errands. She's putting the final touches on the Chapel of the Highest Happiness.

Her first wedding is Friday. The beginning of her ministry.

Kyle and Nick pack me into the back seat of the Volks, my bionic ankle sticking out the passenger window. They wedge my new crutches between the bucket seats. Pin me down.

Nick ties the balloon to my protruding big toe. We peel for West Seattle.

On I-5, the balloon tugs my toe. We hear it snapping madly, and then it breaks free. I watch it drift toward heaven.

"Dude, dude, dude," Kyle keeps saying.

He shakes his head. Grins sublimely.

Kyle has warped the events of graduation night into the parting of the Red Sea, the second coming of Jesus.

But it's safe to say, we made history. I'm not sure what kind of history. But we made it.

Nick hands me the *Seattle Times*. It has commemorated my performance with a photo and an article on page B-1. The photo shows me swinging on the Ric above stage.

The headline reads:

"Daring Young Man on Flying Guitar."

I have mixed feelings about this. I have never sought attention, but somehow it finds me.

I like the picture, though.

The article quotes Miss Yan-Ling:

"Theater is all about magic. When you reach into the hat, you want to pull out something that surprises, shocks, and vivifies. These boys . . . well, Houdini would be proud."

Kyle is also quoted:

"We choreographed everything down to the last detail. We didn't plan for Jonathan to break his leg, or the guitar to explode, but everything else, dude, was in the script."

The article names Kyle as "segment producer."

It ends with a quote from Birdwell: "Jonathan and crew have driven every last atom of pomp out of the Kenny G for a generation to come."

As we drive home, Kyle and Nick fill me in. Gupti is coming around, they say. Rising like a phoenix from the smoking embers of her anger. Except for her and a few faculty members who had to dive out of the way of the falling Kong, the word on my performance is "brilliant."

"Ricky's going into that glass case, all right," Nick says. "Gupti doesn't want to get it repaired. Just display it all charred and fried."

"It's a Hindu thing," Kyle says. "You know, sacrifice on a pyre and all that."

"And she wants to do a photo exhibit—pictures of you and Kong," Nick says. "With a framed copy of the article. And a photo of Telly, of course. And one of The Vedder. Tell the whole story. With Ricky as the centerpiece."

Kyle's grin is wider than his bucket seat.

"Dudes," he says, "we have much to be humble about. For Jonathan will be with us next year."

"Of course," Nick says.

We bump fists all around.

From the back window, I can still see the balloon, a pinprick in the sky.

I close my eyes.

Let the June air rush between my toes, funnel down my cast.

Wash me.

Scrub me.

• • •

When I get home, there's a letter waiting for me on the kitchen table.

From a law firm: Olson, Johnston & Reed.

I circle the table. Nudge the letter suspiciously with the rubber tip of my crutch. Study it from different angles.

I'm pretty sure Gupti and the school district are suing me for damages to the Ric.

It's worth a fortune, and I have now destroyed it. Destroyed the greatest guitar ever, the beautiful cherry red Ric 360-6, The Vedder's gift to Seattle Public Schools. The Vedder's tribute to Telly.

Even putting a low estimate on the value of the Ric, I see myself paying this off for the rest of my life.

I tear open the letter.

Dear Jonathan,

You have been named a beneficiary in the will of my late client, David O. H. Cosgrove II.

Please call me at your earliest convenience. I will be happy to give you the details.

Sincerely,

Ansel T. Reed

Attorney-at-law

chapter 40

Today I'm wearing my charcoal jacket and an old white dress shirt. I'm also wearing a tie.

I'm standing in the back of the Chapel of the Highest Happiness. Leaning on my crutches.

Mimi is swathed in some funky white robe. Belted with a gold ribbon. Preaching a gobbledygook avalanche of Bible verses and Native American Mother Earth metaphors.

Plus her own insights into universal love.

The happy couple doesn't seem to mind.

They stand in stupefied bliss.

A guy named J.R. Big-eared. Sweating.

A woman named Rhonda. Bulb-nosed. Bulb-assed.

Beaming the high beam of the bride.

Small cluster of family and friends.

Mimi pronounces them "husband and wife, a universal unit."

J.R. and Rhonda kiss. Everyone claps.

Mimi presents the marriage certificate. They sign, and she gets a check.

Damn! She's in business.

chapter 41

Today is June 21—the solstice.

Sun gliding near to Earth.

Longest day of the year.

I'm in a new cast. Smaller than the old one, only knee high. A black Velcro-strapped, oversize moon boot.

Leaning on my crutches at the bus stop in the sun. Waiting for the 22.

At the Junction, I swap to the 128. Hobble downhill. Cross the bridge over Schmitz Park. Stop. Gaze down at the creek. The biggest ache I feel today is in my armpits. So I gaze at the creek the way everybody else does. For the sheer beauty and the music of it.

A banner stretches across the dining room of the Delphi:

"Happy 100th Birthday, Agnes!"

Balloons. Party hats. Kazoos.

Big rectangular cake with one fat candle sculpted into the number 100.

All the residents show up. Those who can get around, anyway.

Agnes's daughter, grandchildren, great-grandchildren. Flat Ass and the rest of the staff.

Agnes sits in the center. We sing "Happy Birthday."

She blows out the candle.

Big applause.

Opens her gifts.

One gift is a pair of angel wings that Katie has constructed out of metal hangers and a filmy white curtain liner.

Katie places a loop around Agnes's neck. This attaches the wings to her back.

"Now you really are an angel," Katie says.

Agnes glows.

I hope she'll say it. I even pray for it.

My prayer is answered.

"Float a turd."

While everybody's eating cake and jabbering away, I go to a corner table, open my little notebook:

Chaos XXXI
Deep in the dungeon
the blind man turns my cage,
points toward the chink in the wall.
"Look—LOOK!"
Daylight is leaking in,
drop by drop,
wave by wave.
"Take a deep breath, and go."
So I open the cage,
unlocked all this time.
And push off.
Behind me,
I see only darkness
and no turning back.
To live is to swim toward the shimmer.
To die is to never try.

• • •

Katie tucks Agnes in. Turns on the TV. Settles on *Real Malibu Moms.* Adjusts the standing fan. Dims the lights.

Jeezus! One hundred years old!

Out in the corridor, I hang my backpack on the handlebars of Agnes's wheelchair, plop down in the seat. Lift my moon-booted foot into the silver stirrup.

Katie rolls me into the lobby. Grabs her gray cross-country hoodie. Ties it around her neck.

Places a cap on her bald head.

Places an oxygen bottle in her shoulder bag.

Then she wheels me out the front door of the Delphi, down the ramp.

Into the blue of early evening.

We ease down the hill toward Alki Beach.

On the first day of summer.

Maximal light.

Chilly, breezy, warm.

Typical June in West Seattle.

On the beach, they're building bonfires.

Tangy-salt smell of Puget Sound.

Ketchupy-salt smell of french fries, wafting over from Pepperdock's.

Kids everywhere. From Taft High School and every other school.

Swaggering. Clustering.

Sitting on driftwood logs, thumbing phones. Tight tops. Short shorts. Butt-lows. Toe rings. Skateboards. Frisbees. Volleyballs. iPods.

Immortality.

A river of hogs and open cruisers flows down Beach Drive.

Inevitable cop car, serpent of Eden.

Traveling by wheelchair in this crowd isn't exactly cool. But I'm practicing dude humility, which may be rooted in Buddhism and other ancient religions and philosophies. I'll have to look into that. Maybe there's a poem there.

Quite a few kids come up to me. Ooh and aah over my swinging performance on the Ric.

"Dude, great show! How *did* you do that magic?"

"I had a lot of help," I say.

"You sure played that guitar, man!"

"Nah," I say. "Not really."

I hop to a bench.

Katie sits beside me.

We stare at the shimmering waves.

"Every moment of light and dark is a miracle," Katie says.

Her words flit across my mind like a hummingbird.

"Jeez, Jonathan, I thought you'd get that—Walt Whitman."

Whoa!

Every moment of light and dark is a miracle.

Old Walt coming through.

Channeling.

He may be right. Who knows how many good days we have in us. But there are miracles in moments.

"How *did* you play like that?" Katie asks.

"Luck, I guess."

She ponders this.

I slip my backpack off the handlebars. Unzip it. Pull out my newest purchase. Straight off eBay. Arrived this morning. Total cost, including tax and postage: $972.

But I'm not sweating it.

"What's that?"

I reach into my pocket for a pick. Find one among the pennies and dimes.

"A lute."

Then I say, "Handcrafted in Bulgaria in 1919. Check this out."

I smooth my hand over the teardrop-shaped solid spruce soundboard, the gourdlike back, up the ebony neck to the ornamented headstock. But the sound hole is coolest—cut in the shape of a grand cathedral window.

"Can you play it?" Katie asks.

I tuck into the little instrument. Try an open arpeggio. Sounds like a rusty day in hell.

Ancient, twangy.

A retarded banjo.

"I have no idea how to play this," I say.

I'm pretty sure I'm gonna kiss her.

When it gets dark.

But *damn!* It's the longest day of the year.

"You'll figure it out," she says.